The Giulio METAPHYSICS III

The Giulio

META PHYS ICS III

Michael Mirolla

Leapfrog Press
Fredonia, New York

The Giulio Metaphysics III © 2013 by Michael Mirolla
All rights reserved under International and
Pan-American Copyright Conventions

Published in 2013 in the United States by
Leapfrog Press LLC
PO Box 505
Fredonia, NY 14063
www.leapfrogpress.com

Printed in the United States of America

Distributed in the United States by
Consortium Book Sales and Distribution
St. Paul, Minnesota 55114
www.cbsd.com

First Edition

ISBN: 978-1-935248-39-2

Library of Congress Cataloging-in-Publication Data

CIP data available from the Library of Congress

the
place
to
find
the

(center)

is
at
the
edge

—Charles Bukowski ("the happy life of the tired")

Acknowledgements

The following stories have been previously published, some in revised form:

The Battered Suitcase:	"Triptych"
Arabesques:	"Into another kind of country"
Canadian Fiction Magazine:	"Giulio's farewell (or the extrapolation blues)"
	"Giulio dans le metro"
	"Giulio's mother"
	"The man in the basement"
	"The hyperboreans: a re-enactment"
	"A general introduction to pure phenomenology"
EVENT magazine:	"Giulio in the country"
Italian-Canadian Anthology:	"Giulio visits a friend"
Prairie Journal:	"Giulio upon his wife"

"This is the story of Crow," "This is a Raven story," "Pima Oriole Song 47": Excerpted from *Coming to Light: Contemporary Translations of the Native Literatures of North America*, Brian Swann, ed. (Vintage 1996).

"The Mass of Interment": Excerpt from *Dies Irae*, from the Mass of the Dead.

Contents

PROLOGUE: Signing on

I fall.

Tumbling head over heels. Arms flailing. Legs scissoring. No longer trapped within the boxy confines of the genre. Within the strictures that have tied and bound. Within the artifice and limiting parameters of the written-on-the-blank-tablet message.

I fall.

Tossing pages to the left and right. Up and down. Fragments of words, phrases, sentences. Accordion-like pieces of paragraphs that stretch away from me in an attempt to escape before snapping back into my face. Before parading military-style in front of my eyes. Before stuffing themselves into my mouth.

I fall.

Hoping to escape. To make a clean getaway. But the words are insistent. They insist on being read. They insist on being swallowed. They insist on being turned into flesh. They will not leave me alone. They demand a sacrifice. They want to nail me to the wall. Keep me fixed forever.

I fall instead.

Insisting in turn: "It's the falling that keeps me free." The mantra that I keep repeating as my arms flail and my legs scissor and I tumble head over heels.

But I know it can't go on forever. I can't keep falling forever. The words will catch up to me. And they will crucify me.

In the meantime.

I.

Fall.

Families, Friendlies, Familiars I

I. Giulio's mother

Giulio's mother, I write in my cramped style, in my cramped, ever-so-peculiar style, Giulio's mother showed him the reality in dreams. For that, Giulio vows, she can never be forgiven, must never be absolved. Condemned forever to these pages, she is caught between the moment her hand connected with his face and her inevitable collapse in the ensuing shockwave. A slow crumple on to the unyielding sidewalk, preceded by a sigh that pierced him like a rusty stiletto. That jammed itself down his throat like an infernally-twisted and hookwormed clothes-hanger. That yanked out his guts and his bloodied pride and left them both shriveling in the hot sun.

Why, oh why? he finds himself asking. Why did she do it? Why did she permit such an absence to take place? Do curses grope blindly about until they find someone to whom they can attach themselves, with whom they become enamoured, against whom they forcibly meld? To start all over as one reluctant, ungainly creature—tripping across itself, stumbling forward, the sutures constantly coming undone, the wound ever bleeding? In dreams they do; in stupors; in trances: the heart's very own personal electro-magnetic field.

Giulio is in a dream, I proceed to write from inside my restraining—yet at the same time protective—enclosure. In a stupor. In a trance. Has just finished a bowl of strawberries and sour cream. The streets of Park Ex, pedestrian at best, suddenly glow with decadence. And secrecy. Hushed whispers. Whispering breezes. A faint radioactive sparkle with a faint radioactive pulse along the grim edges of the horizon. There are murmurs everywhere; rumours and boarders in the air. Even the clouds go against the grain. Grist for my mill. Water under the bridge. Psst! Did you hear? Mrs. Kowalsky's husband had been acquainted with a czar, had been among the crowd that trampled decorum and Jews to touch his sacred hem, to be pleasing in his eyes. Really? Scout's honour. Well, to tell the truth, Mrs. Kowalsky's husband wasn't actually to blame—a mere spoilt brat in knee breeches at the time—but he sleeps clutching a tattered red rag under his pillow. A Tatar-ed read flag? No bull. The alleys slide furtively into the maw of the setting sun. Sunbeams gathering all light and bringing it back to the mother ship. A pinball tilt. Illegitimate use of the laws of physics and gravity. But it's all allowed. In a dream. In a stupor. In a trance. With a mighty crackle and an even mightier rending, the buildings rise on their staunch hind legs, spraying to mark the dusty territory. A dusky fairy story? The sabre-toothed buses eat up the distance, leaving both exhaust and exhaustion behind. The priest, rake-thin and freshly-blooded from his daily self-scourging, throws open the haunted portals. He's hoping to stir up interest. Or trouble. To send out the spirited emissaries on waves of heat-layered air. But the real question is: Will they themselves return—or will they too be lost in those endlessly furtive alleys, filled with the carcasses of rotting cats and debutantes' shoes?

Who could fail to comment on the personification of a Park Ex summer, especially in a dream? The liquid over-brimming as teary eyes slowly shut? The pang in the gut from a semi-continent of lack of continence? The asphalt macadam dry heave melting of the stoniest heart? Not Giulio, certainly. Certainly, not Giulio. Giulio, certainly not.

Don't look back, I scribble without malice aforethought, my writing now practically impossible to decipher where all the lines meet in the cubicle's far corner. You can never tell what blessed monsters you're ignoring, red-faced and frustrated; what deep caverns and solicitudes with mouths agape you're leaving in your blissful wake. A dream is all dread and ahead. All free-fall fast-forward. All blur and fuzz. A blank tape ready for fitful recording. And re-recording. The over-dub reality. A re-writable blue-tinged DVD. Just click on the right button and it'll play it all back for you, freeze frame by freeze frame.

"Say there, big Giulio. What gives, eh? Haven't seen ya in a month of Sundays. Where ya been to do your sin?"

The voice calls from the edge of a rooftop, from a shadow that manoeuvres its chariot wheelchair ever-so-dexterously across the chasms, rims spinning lightly in the air.

"Greetings, Pagan." Looking up. Squinting, sun in his eyes. Glint of some scarab with a multiplexed chest protector. Giulio tries to put up his own guard just in case. Too late. Any street fighter's well-handled sword would have slipped right through the chain-mail chinks, bursting open the no-tell-tale heart within. "Youth Council tomorrow?"

"Just the execs." The Pagan man spirals down to street level, the twin ramps surging ahead, then vanishing behind him. "So where ya goin', huh? Pool hall? Girl? Com' on. You can tell me. Mum's the word."

"Just the execs?" Still squinting, teary-eyed.

The crunch of gravel under aluminum wheels. A spin; a twirl; up on one rim; then back like a bucking bronco. Giulio claps, fits two fingers into his mouth and lets out a shrill whistle.

"Thank you. Thank you." A bow from the waist. From such a waste? There is no more beneath that blanket. Nothing that functions. Just take a peek, if you dare. A wasted waist. Like a falling off at the edge of the known universe. "Yeah, just the execs. You know? The ones in charge of drawing up the high and mighty constitution. Where ya goin'? Mind if I tag along, huh?"

Giulio shrugs. I make a note: All ahead in a dream, all encounter and lack of. Sometimes two people pass right through each other, or fit into each other perfectly for a moment—child, young man, pre-adult, post-adult, doddering old fool with a useless wisdom tooth and a diddle for a cock-a-doodle-doo—and then slip out once more. And, miracle of miracles, they can do this time and time again, thumbing their noses at Descartes. At old, three-D bound cracked leather-faced Descartes. But only in a dream. Otherwise, you just bump together and that's that.

Can that really be that? I ask in exegetic pomp, scribbling against the steamed-up bathroom wall. In the folly of pompous youth. Under circumstances of contingency. Whatever. I continue: The twilight in Park Ex is like a gypsy's eyes—or a drunk's burp. Giulio climbs her stairs on all fours, spiralling upward towards a strawberry-and-sour-creamy Milky Way. One must know one's stars if one is to know one's self. That's the saying, alright. But what about stairs? Are they as important, as seminal? Does one extra letter, one extra step, make all that much difference? Don't you need stairs to get to stars? More questions: Do you love walks in the park, in a sex-glazed piggery where the sharp, coarse grass hides a whiplash intimacy? Fine powdery canine excrement both emerging and crumbling with the spring sun? Ripped-off manhole covers full of hairless tennis balls? The screech of hockey stick slivers on fatally cracked cement? The scrunch of football cleats on dandelion patches? Friends? Ah, friends? Remember friends? Do you love the friends who have nurtured you, incubated you, raised you on their curdled kindness? Giulio wishes he could. Giulio only wishes that it were possible. Even if only for a milli-second. Even if only in a quasi-possibility in some possible world far away. Even if only in an electrified vat.

Up her stairs he crawls, remembering earlier dreams all in a jumble, brushing the sudden nettles from his legs, the evergreen canopy and the buzz of insects, carpets sprouting trees and the musty smells of previous couplings both human and otherwise. Then the hurried slaps and dribbles as the mosquitoes sucked on his buttocks. And the Pagan, scarab-armed, standing guard, ready to take a second bullet for the cause. What about the bed? What about it? Isn't there someone on that bed—half-on half-off? A body folded back in two, feet securely anchored to the floor? Aren't those Giulio's hands contravening the padded nylon, the panting hose? Dinner with a fork? An extra button between his teeth? A bellwether dingaling? And isn't that a twisted, hunch-backed urchin swinging from the chandelier, grinning down at his fumbling, tugging, yanking, bits of flesh coming away, following the line of the nylon run, hissing like acid at the rise in his pleasure?

"Your mother," the urchin shrieks, smashing lights and fine china in his whirling dervish way. In his devilish swirling way. "Hee hee. She's downstairs. Ha ha. She's asking for you. Ho ho."

"My mother? What—"

"She's crying, you know." He covers his eyes. A glint. Peek-a-boo. Mocking. "Tut tut. She's crying. Boo hoo."

And he swings away, bouncing off the walls, rolling like a ball, then springing up perfectly balanced with a suddenly-grown third leg. Stiffly proud.

"Don't go," Pagan whispers to Giulio from a rooftop across the street, in a voice for his ears only. "It's a trick. Nothing but a low-down dirty trick."

I make a note, crooked stick in the sand pile at my feet: No, that's not the trick. The real trick is not to look behind you. Know what I mean? The moon in Park Ex rises just above the Greek cinema. There they once showed horror movies that ended precisely at dusk, that released with filmic ease the two-dimensional monsters to accompany you home. Sucked out from the hyper-reel into the ordinary real—and leaving unmendable gaps in both. Giulio looks back and there she is, silhouetted beneath the moon. The silvery moon. Suddenly old, arms out, slowly collapsing, twisting, thudding, pleading, entreating. Her tears send him careening down the street, send him vomiting into the sidewalk nettles, a steady stream of bile that curls the hardiest of thistles. Giulio vows to hate her forever, to turn her memory black, to mis-shape the muscle of their love. How could he step into that house again? How could he eat a meal under her roof again? That's his blood colouring the thick red sauce, his flesh and bone-marrow flavouring the twined twirled strands that he normally swallows without chewing, feeling them slide down his throat into the pit of his stomach. How could he? He swallows without chewing.

Giulio's mother sits across from him at the kitchen table, I scratch into the soft basement plaster with my bleeding nails, with my ripped-to-shreds cuticles. She sits across from him. Head cradled in her arms. Eyes rimmed rabbit pink with self-pity. The knowledge of victory in that sweet heart of hearts. The knowledge to encompass all pain.

And the pain to encompass all knowledge.

II. The man in the basement

The man in the basement, a half-empty wine glass in his pale-blue hand, has just died. He might easily have been someone's father. Or a former prisoner of war. Or an oven tender on the night shift in a pastry shop. That he hated weapons—even toy ones—and, in the morning, brought home day-old doughnuts for his children was no guarantee of his identity. But it did help establish what he was not. He was not German though he knew some German expressions learnt under duress. He was not young. He was not happy. Except perhaps when in his basement, surrounded by the alchemy of fermentation, the juice that, transmuted to a clear unclouded ruby, flowed through his veins—and back out again. Or in his garden where he trod like a shrunken god working earthwormy magic, the loam turned to gold in his hands.

"Otherwise, he was a failure," I have Giulio readily admit as he watches his body no longer twitch violently, a twitch that had been with him even in the deepest sleep—as if always ready for a blow that might come at any moment and from any angle. "He could display no affection. Feared the coming of glandular old age. Cursed past and present with the same dour breath. His pride sat on him like a giant toad, devouring everything that came near. He fought with everyone, made enemies with a flippant slip of the tongue. Often, he kept bitterness deep within, in a secret compartment, letting it ferment and bubble over into strong vinegar. And then he lashed out at his wife, at us, at the neighbours, at the relatives near and far, at the moon and the stars, at the whole damned carousel of things. The most familiar pose had him with his back to me, leaning against the rear screen door, one arm on his hip, the other on the splintering wooden frame, staring out at the blanket darkness of the back fields. As if out there was the answer, out there the response to a question he dare not even repeat out loud."

And yet, consummate grafter of old and new, of yin and yang, he was capable of miracles. Of true creation. That much must be noted. So noted. From between his fingers, figs and peaches escaped into the relentless Canadian winter. Grapes hung from trellises like the fat exclamation points in a melodrama. Daily, bell peppers sizzled in the frying pan; cherry tomatoes added gilt to cold-cut sandwiches; pears and apples clung in desperation to scraggly limbs, fruits often too heavy for their puny bearers, fruits so over-bearing they sometimes had to be propped up by the judicious use of sawed-off hockey sticks.

"When he drank," Giulio continues, having been made to feel suddenly confessional, "the middle road was not for him. Instead, he would careen down one of two paths, one of two extremes. He might become overly generous, full of guffaws, gentility and god-awful jokes. Or instantly vicious. Someone might, in passing, mention his mother—taken in this case as a neutral object in the experiment. If in a generous mood, she was a beautiful Madonna who raised eight children on nothing but sweat and crushing work, who never complained the earth was hard, that the life of an Italian peasant prepared a person well for hell. If vicious, she was a careless bitch who had never been grateful for what he had done, for his sacrifices as the eldest, who had given away his property, his due, who had. . . . There followed mad rushes and slamming of doors, cruel epithets hurled at his children who shivered in their beds, curses heaped on his wife. Why? Tell me that. Why?"

Why? I repeat just to make sure I understand correctly. Why as in 'why'? Or as in 'Y', the two paths forking, and then diverging forever in an ever-expanding universe? Perhaps, only to meet at some—

"No, fuck!" Giulio says, exploding, clenched fist about to slam the side of the coffin. "A simple why will do, thank you. And an even simpler response. Just this once."

—At some point along the line of infinite digression, I finish the thought. Giulio lowers his head.

"A simple why," he mutters under his breath.

But I have no simple why's to give. No wise and none the wiser. So let's move on, shall we?

What other questions might be answered instead: How is wine made—honestly, that is, and with grapes? Is the grafting of a delicate

vine on to sturdy stock good or bad? What is the correct temperature and humidity for the keeping of fine sausage, cured ham, pick-
led beet? How deeply must a fig-tree be buried so that winter doesn't
shrivel it up, the succulence like an ante-diluvian memory never to
be revived?

"One time," Giulio recounts in the dim, respectful light, grinding
his teeth (not unlike the old man now lying before him), "suspecting
some secret kept back from him or perhaps some secret inadvertently
told him, he attacked my mother with a knife, a huge meat cleaver he
sharpened each day on a whetstone in the basement. There was absolutely no humanity in him, only the desire to do away with something. Anything. Other people's love, perhaps; the cutting edge of
emotion; the magical barrier he couldn't cross for fear of making
a fool of himself. And my mother, always one for the grand effect,
exposing her breast, egged him on, urged him to strike, to sink the
knife as deep as possible into her. Naturally, he couldn't. His rage
was all an act, an act so choked with weeds that by the time it surfaced
. . . ah, you know what I mean? If ever I had the chance to hit him, it
was then: poor helpless, knife-wielding creature; poor trudger over
virgin snow, the moonlight infinitely more vicious than he could
ever dream of being, exposing every line, every flaw, every grey hair
that burst out in the middle of the night, breath vaporizing, nose
blanching."

More questions: How many lovers—half-on half-off—bled into
one another as he made his journey downtown? How many drunks
stumbled by on their way to plonk blankness and nirvana? How
many incomprehensible whores went round and round the pastry
shop, their noses in the air, sniffing the soft warm delicacies that
he had stood guard over for twenty years, the dough untouched by
human hands? Who needs it? Was it then new vine shoots sprouted
in the garden, like the fast-forward on a VCR? Was it then tomatoes ripened, spilling red across the yellow Formica table top? Was it
then heliotropes popped, scanned the heavens in search of their real
roots, roots left behind in a pastel-coloured Mediterranean village?
Was it then the blood-wine bubbled merrily over the demi-john lips
onto the floor of the cantina, proud of its drinkability? Of his drink
abilities?

"That night, I should have hit him," Giulio says to himself, fist clenched once more, as he leans over and kisses him on the coldest of foreheads, unfurrowed at last. "I should have pummelled him and maybe even kicked him a couple of times when he was down. I should have sunk my boot between his collapsing ribs, into his rotting gut, beneath his shrunken jaw. Yeah, that's what I should have done. It would have made it possible for me to love him at last." He looks up at the makeshift altar, at the candles burning with electric flames, at the wreath bidding him farewell. "Don't you think?"

When he asks questions like that, you know I can only shrug.

I shrug.

III. The hyperboreans: a re-enactment

*[Offstage: Anxious **Playwright/Director** pacing back and forth in the shadows. Wringing his hands. Looking up at the sky as if for guidance. Occasionally peering out from behind the curtains. Then, resuming his pacing.]*

*[Onstage: A street corner set to simulate a rundown neighbourhood. Perhaps once middle-class but no longer. Two-dimensional storefronts—ice eating away at the shoddy brickwork. Lighting dim as eternal twilight. Valhalla. Snow. **Giulio**, standing. **Pagan**, sitting in wheelchair. Both frozen, staring off-stage somewhere. Have been standing/sitting that way for one thousand years. Or a single Zeno moment. Without warning, they stir. Come to life as if nothing has happened. As if no time has passed. As if simply continuing their conversation.]*

GIULIO

(leaning against the soft underbelly of one more winter's twilight)

I was saying Park Ex has much to be proud of. What say you, Pagan, my boy? So unrosy-fingered at this time of day.

*[**Pagan** shifts his weight on the wheelchair, fearing a sudden lack of sensation and the permanent stiffness in his lower back where the bullet had entered.]*

PAGAN

(blowing out a cloud of air for effect—and then blowing on his exposed fingers)

Hey, it's getting fucking cold. That's what I say. How's about dropping into Valois for a game—and a brew or two?

GIULIO

Anything you say.

(Giulio looks up and down the street. Up and down the street.)

I'm ready to follow you anywhere. Let's go.

[They don't move, although there is a hint of shuffling, just a touch of molecular stirring. Behind the store-front window, a tiny lady in spectacles—a spectrum of pins jutting from her mouth—begins to strip the mannequins. They, too, don't move, although the indignity must affect them. Deep down having to stand naked and exposed must hurt them—even if the covering of rime makes it hard to look in. Acts as a sort of virginal dress, all lacy and discreet yet at the same time enticing.]

GIULIO

You know, Pagan, my boy, Park Ex has always been considered the veritable armpit of the city—

PAGAN

No, no. You got it all wrong. That's the East End.

GIULIO

The East End? Hmm . . . come to think of it, you might be right, my boy. The arse hole, then. How's that?

PAGAN

The stinking, puckered-up arse hole, for sure. And the inhabitants are useful in the occasional wiping of it.

GIULIO

That's the general consensus, the noise bruited about. But me, I've been living here 30 years now—

PAGAN

Christ! Has it really been that long? Giulio, say it ain't so.

[Pagan spins around in the snow, leaving strange indecipherable tracks that move forward slightly before completing the ragged circle. Snow circles. Can aliens be far behind?]

GIULIO

Thirty years. And you know something?

PAGAN

What?

GIULIO

You know something?

PAGAN

What, Giulio? What?

GIULIO

I've . . . I've . . . I've lost my train of thought.

[A cardboard bus pulls up reluctantly to the corner, squealing to an icy stop as it slips sideways. Women scramble from every nook and cranny to climb aboard—a babble of tongues and yoked eye-brows, flesh form-fitted into the meat-grinder.]

PAGAN

Look at that, will ya?

(rubs his ears and knocks snow from the woolen blanket covering his legs)

Another day over at the pyramids. And now rushing back to prepare supper for their husbands who, parting polluted seas, rush to them from the other side, knives and forks in hand.

GIULIO

Pyramids?

(removes a glove and scratches his head, indicating confusion)

What pyramids?

[The bus picks itself up, back-fires twice and disappears in a puff of black smoke.]

PAGAN

The goddam Egyptian pyramids. You know. Is there any other kind? They're square at the bottom. But somehow, at the end of it all, they manage to come to a point. To the point.

GIULIO

Listen, Pagan, you don't have to tell me about the pyramids. Or coming to the point. I once knew all about the Riddle of the Sphinx—and in capital letters, too. But these women are mostly Greeks and Wops. And they do piece-work in garment factories owned mostly by Jews. Where do the Egyptians come into the picture?

PAGAN

Giulio, Giulio.

(shakes his head—most sadly)

Listen to yourself talk. Use your imagination, why don't you?

GIULIO

I'm trying. Believe me, I'm trying. If I close my eyes—

(shuts his eyes)

Yeah, you're right—if I close my eyes, I can pretend this stuff flying around, burning my face, is the grittiest sand. And the crackling beneath my feet is the grist of countless wheat mills. And isn't that the patchwork Nile in the distance, quilty and silted? And . . . and . . .

so what if it's twenty-five below and my cock's about to fall off into my boots . . . and—

PAGAN

Okay, okay, wise guy. Point made and noted.

> [Pagan slaps the sides of the wheelchair, unsheathing two circles of ice that shatter as they hit the ground. Giulio lifts his collar and slips his neck a little deeper into the regulation pea-coat, the standard Park Ex garb for this particular thousand-year reign. Behind him, he catches a glimpse of a proto-woman in a strapless gold bra. She is definitely bald but in no way embarrassed.]

How's the ex-, Giulio?

GIULIO

(looks away—far, far away)

Fine, I guess. Last I heard she was living somewhere in the wilds of Ontario.

PAGAN

And the kid? How she doin'?

GIULIO

What is this: twenty questions?

PAGAN

Just tryin' to make conversation, is all.

GIULIO

The kid? The kid's fine, too, I guess. A great skater from what I hear. A regular . . . what's the name? . . . Fleming. Yeah, a regular Peggy Fleming.

PAGAN

Whew! For a moment I thought you were about to say Reggie. Now, there's someone Park Ex can really be proud of.

GIULIO

Sure, Pagan. Greatest player to ever put on a pair of skates—and then proceed to lace them together.

PAGAN

Giulio, it hurts me to say this but life's turned you into a pessimist.

GIULIO

What! And after I said Park Ex had a lot to be proud of. That's the thanks I get. Oh, it doesn't pay to be a prophet in your own land.

> [A shard of ice-laden wind rips down the constantly shrinking street, seemingly in an attempt to close off both ends. Pagan

stiffens. The two shuffle less and less, the molecules gelatinous, like thick soup. Soon, they'll become visible, floating in the air like loose pieces of Styrofoam wrapping.]

PAGAN

Okay, okay. Maybe pessimist's too strong a word. Cynic, then. How's that?

GIULIO

Thanks a lot. Thanks a mighty bunch. That's like saying I wouldn't spit at my mother but I wouldn't put it past you to spit at yours.

PAGAN

Oh yeah?

GIULIO

Yeah!

[They both turn and look in opposite directions. There's a long meaningful pause.]

Pagan, what are we doing standing here? Just what the hell are we doing standing here?

PAGAN

Speak for yourself. I only wish I were standing here.

[They turn to face each other again.]

GIULIO

Shit. I need a drink; you need a drink; Park Ex needs a drink. A long, fucking stiff one. One that never ends. An eternal drink. Mead forever pouring down the gullet. In a land where the only breeze brings the odor of paradise.

PAGAN

Me, I need someone to make decisions for me.

GIULIO

And to buy me a villa on an Egyptian island. Right next to the Sphinx.

PAGAN

Say, Mister Giulio, can you spare a dream?

GIULIO

I've got plenty of dreams. Too many to juggle. Maybe I should get myself a dream broker—to tell me which dream stock is rising and which about to take a sudden nose-dive. They know about such things—and they're always one step ahead of mere mortals. Playing the margins, I think they call it. Sell those dreams before they turn into nightmares.

PAGAN

Things will be different in the spring. You wait and see.

GIULIO

We have little choice.

> *[Too late they notice the street lights, the fluttering pools of snow, the dark cutting edge of winter night.]*

You know, Pagan. Someone watching us would think we were two lost souls adrift on the sea of life. Unable and unwilling to find their way home. How wrong they'd be. How totally off-base.

PAGAN

Yeah. We're pretty solidly anchored, ain't we? Especially as this sea is frozen over—and we've been left stuck in it up to our ankles.

> *[The store lights blink and go out. The spectacled lady locks the door behind her, tugging with all her might to make sure it clicks shut. Pagan smiles at her but she sees right through him and disappears into the thickening blizzard.]*

How about my place?

> *[Pagan moves his arms in slow-motion like stiff windmills.]*

GIULIO

(shrugs)

Sure. What's on TV?

PAGAN

A classic. 'Hercules vs. The Thing From The Mausoleum'. A genuine, fucking classic.

GIULIO

Damn. I've seen it.

> *[Giulio swivels robot-like to face the other way. Then tilts his head to the sky and opens his mouth. But the flakes veer away from him, almost as if they're afraid of what they'll find in that outwardly inviting maw.]*

PAGAN

You sure?

GIULIO

Absolutely, Mr. Pagan. Not likely to forget a genuine, fucking classic like that, am I?

PAGAN

Sure it wasn't 'Hercules vs. The Creature From Atlantis'—another genuine classic?

GIULIO

Positive. I remember the big boy unwrapping the mummy.

PAGAN

You mean his mummy, don't you?

GIULIO

No, I mean *the* mummy, dummy. One strand at a time.

(pauses, breathing out fiercely)

Oh, what the hell! I wouldn't mind seeing it again. Let's go.

[And Giulio reaches forward to grip the back of the wheelchair, to give it the gentle shove it needs to get going. And, real-life Zeno, never quite makes it. And will now have to wait another thousand years to come to life again. Deep freeze. Lights down. Shadowy figure looks this way and that. Then picks up the two cardboard cutouts and walks off with them.]

IV. A general introduction to pure phenomenology

The porcelain cup out of which Giulio is sipping coffee once contained arsenic (a thousand years ago perhaps—or yesterday). And will again someday. But no one knows when—not even me. Or if there's a pattern to the fillings and emptyings. He swallows slowly, in tiny gulps, fingers wrapped around the greasy, battle-scarred container, letting the coffee drip organically into his half-awakened mind.

He swallows and waits for the poison to take effect. Poor Giulio. Alas, there's no arsenic in the muddy mixture he drinks this particular morning. Not the least trace. He holds the cup close to his eye and stares into the dregs, not noticing the wheelchair circling behind him.

"You'll meet a fair-haired, rosy-cheeked, toga-clad youth who'll take you home with him and shyly introduce you to his parents." Pagan laughs as he reaches across to pat Giulio on the back. "Hey, what the hell were you doing last night, anyway? Chasing butterflies? I looked all over the place for you."

"Last night?" Giulio shakes the cup, hoping for a different configuration. No such luck. "Listen, Pagan, my boy. Last night I was untouched by human hands. Last night I was St. Peter staggering down a rut-infested road singing: 'As I was a-walking down Paradise Street, To me Aye Aye, Blow the man down!' Do you know it, perchance?"

"Of course not. In case you hadn't noticed, I've a crippled imagination, atrophied from non-use. Paradise Street slipped away from me a long, long time ago."

Pagan swings his wheelchair around, butting it up against the table. Outside, through the greasy spoon's plate-glass window, the dawn makes itself known with grey-speckled snowflakes. Ashy and bitter to the taste. A man, only lunch box and breath visible, is bundled by, hurried along by a decidedly ferocious wind.

"Now, that man," Pagan declaims, suddenly pointing, "is chasing butterflies. I'm absolutely positive. Do you want to hear my theory on butterflies?"

"*Cameriere*," Giulio shouts and holds up his cup. "Another coffee. And this time hold the mud, *per piacere*."

"Here it is then. Pagan the Cripple's theory: Butterflies were meant to be chased. When they flutter over the piss-yellow flowers, the gnarly-burly thorns, they want nothing but a boy with a net bounding behind them. A boy with two strong legs, with suddenly no father, no past, a boy whose mind stretches no further than the last bruised butterfly spinning in ever-diminishing circles around the milkweed. I bet you didn't know that. I bet that's something that slipped your mind."

"Who you trying to kid, Pagan? Slipped my mind, indeed. I have a graduate degree in butterfly-chasing."

"Oh yeah?"

"Sure. The first one I ever caught ended up pregnant. Have you ever been chained to a pregnant butterfly?"

"I don't like the turn this conversation has taken."

"Go to hell then. It's obvious your grasp of butterflies is superficial. Powder-puff stuff. Simple nostalgia for slow-motion jaunts through sunflower fields."

Giulio sips his fresh coffee. He sniffs, trying desperately to inhale. Something. Anything. I write: Isn't that the odour of bitter almonds? Gutted peach stones? Wishful thinking. Oh dear old dad. When he died, they covered his eyes with plum pits and braided a necklace of sour grapes to hide the scars. Did you love him, man? There are plenty of null sets to be filled. Or only one repeated endlessly to contain all the emptiness in the universe—including itself. Emptiness containing emptiness. You have a choice: the many emptinesses or the one. For the Zen Buddhist in all of us.

"Giulio, I'm gonna become a detective."

"That's good 'cause you're half-way there."

"Huh? What's that supposed to mean?"

"Just change the first 't' to an 'f'."

"Up yours, man! I make up up here what I ain't got down there. Anyway, I got it all worked out. I'll hook on to one of the masters, one of the great ones. He'll show me the—don't you say it! Don't you dare!—he'll show me the ropes. After that, it'll be a cinch, all down-hill. I'll wander about—here, let me read the promotional material for you—'in the murky night, crystal daggers everywhere, through deep almost infinite alleys, in search of the last innocent man on earth. The last Sir Galahad.' Good, eh?"

"Can you handle a gun? Or a mistress?"

"Giulio, Giulio. What a pathetic, backward notion you have of detectives. Don't you know they've got lackeys for that kind of shit-ass stuff?"

Giulio shrugs. Pagan nods. A man and a woman step without hesitation into a three-foot snowdrift. They laugh. His hand reaches inside her coat, inside the warmth, the comfort zone where . . . Ah, forget it, dear boy. That's the laughter of madness, of mutual insani-ty. What about quilts on a winter night, a warm dank body rising in joyous quivers? A hand lifting the tattered lace curtain. There, in the shadow of barnyard and snowflakes, something pawing at the latest crust of ice, dashing madly across the daguerreotype. Perfect. That's enough light. Too much and the effect is spoiled, over-exposed. De-tective, detective. Giulio has a half-riddle for you. He wants you to—no, it's too too silly, too far gone. Her belly a little larger than abso-lutely necessary, pan-shaped, full. Mining for gold. He dives beneath the quilt—a seeker after pearls, perhaps. Or one particular pearl. Fleshy button between his teeth. In the muffled heat, her breath comes as heavily as . . . as a huge red beast leaping repeatedly against the farmhouse door. Inside, his mate, tiny and neurotic, shaking, lies curled next to the wood stove.

"Let him in," she says, drawing back her breath in the tingly after-math. "I'll put some coffee on."

Giulio lies in a pool of something damp. And corrosive. Let's call it the oxidation of life. For simplicity's sake. Rust-bucket sex. Na-ked, she sways gently towards an understanding. The dog rushes in, hurling snow as it snake-dances across the floor. A child stirs in an upstairs crib, clapboard creaking. The flies, interned in the walls, prepare to tumble out at the first sign of warmth. Programmed to tumble out.

"What do you want to hear?" he asks, his body inverted and dis-torted in a crystal cut glass jug. "The 'Ninth' or 'Highway Sixty-One Revisited'? Your choice."

He waits a moment. Then calls out again when there's no re-sponse. But she is gone, having stepped out through the farmhouse roof, child in her arms. Like some rustic Madonna in her ascension. All he has left is the smell of coffee perking on the pot-bellied stove. And the scratchy album caught in one shredded groove, unable to make the jump from 'Ode To Joy' to 'Black Crows In The Meadow'. Later, the smell of coffee burning, coffee caramelizing really: a black-ened residue at the bottom of the pot no amount of scraping will ever remove. And unreadable.

"You know, Giulio my man, there's nothing quite like these ear-ly-morning conversations over stale coffee and yesterday's even stal-er doughnuts." Pagan searches through the newspaper, also a left-over from the previous day. "They clear up so many things. Don't you think?"

"Huh! Oh yeah sure. But I wish they'd clear this table off once in a while. That coffee stain—the one that looks like a rock 'n' roll skull?—that's been here since the first time I walked into this place, flushed from a comic-book raid on Ben's. Ah, I was so much older then. On the other hand, I probably wouldn't recognize the joint without the stains."

"Hey, listen to this, why don't you." Pagan reads: " 'As a man ap-proaches thirty, the testing pattern of his life is about over. He is ready to come to earth.' Hey, I'm one step ahead, having crash-landed al-ready. 'He has selected the career he wants; the wife he craves; the chil-dren he deserves; the home he feels comfortable in. At thirty, a man starts to climb his way up his chosen field of endeavour. He –' " Pagan stops, does a semi-whirl with his wheelchair. "Giulio, what's wrong?"

"Can't you see what's wrong? I'm crying. You sure are a half-assed detective."

"Stop it or you'll have me doing it, too."

"Come on, Pagan. We're stepping out. It's getting mighty stuffy in here."

And that, at least, can't be denied. The windows are being steamed up by the wrinkled, water-logged hot dogs and sizzling burgers, the bubbling pots of spaghetti and tomato sauce, the active sacrilegious breathing of other humans. Giulio reaches across the table and wipes the steam away with his elbow. Again and again. Where is he? Where the hell is he? In the garden, in this particular garden, a diminutive figure hauls away massive, overflowing shovelfuls of snow. He works unhurriedly, without haste. Yet the path is being cleared as if by a cartoon character, darkness sagging about him through the creator's mental lapses. Can he make the pigeon house by nightfall? Is it possible? Someday that man will be positively dead, draped in fig leaves and garlands of sour grapes. Giulio will wipe all the fogged-up windows in the world in search of him. Aha! Hire a detective. And, speak of the devil, there's Pagan on the rooftop, spinning in the midst of a storm. Only the bullet wound is suddenly a fresh one, fountaining blood out of his spine like tomato sauce.

"Leave it to me," Pagan whispers in obvious pain, doubled over, clutching his chest. "I'll find him for you. Don't you worry. I'll bring him back—dead or alive."

Perhaps it's the sound of grapes being pressed that will lead to him? Or the smell of the toilet after he's used it? Or the gurgle of the wine from demi-john to gallon to bottle to glass? But, Giulio, wouldn't you like to pin him down at last, even if you have to step on his head to do it? Or mount him as part of your butterfly collection? Butterfly collection? What butterfly collection?

"Giulio! Giulio!" his mother cries out, dipping a wooden spoon into the thick sauce and stirring to make sure it doesn't stick to the bottom and burn. "What's the matter with you? The door-bell."

He thinks of reaching for the door and it flies open.

"Hello. You made it." She nods, standing in the doorway, peering over his shoulder, green eyes flashing. "Come in. She's waiting for you."

"Listen, Giulio." She takes his hands for a moment. Then let's go again. "I'm scared."

"What's there to be scared about?" he asks, smiling the way he does when he is scared. Or, at least, unsure of himself.

"Your mother—"

"It's all right. It's okay. That day, she didn't understand, that's all. She wasn't herself, that's all."

Is that all? Holding out her arms, wooden spoon in one hand, clove of garlic in the other, his mother smiles. Like a saint. Or a witch. Pagan flies away to a Youth Council meeting, to make executive decisions, to remain forever young. They are taking pot shots at him, calculating the trajectory, waiting to pick him off. But it's no use. He's always one step ahead of their explosions. In the garden the figure shovels a little more quickly, with a little more urgency. The wind has detoured behind him, cutting him off, piling the snow back on the path. But he doesn't care right now. It's all ahead in this dream. He pushes his way into the pigeon house at last. White smoke curls from its make-shift chimney, hard to distinguish from the surrounding snow. What does that mean? What is that smoke a sign of? No Popish plot, we hope? Or stratagems for a division of power? The child Giulio emerges suddenly from the castle, a hump of snow on his back. Already the wind has covered all trace of footsteps—and the assassins have slipped away again, gliding effortlessly, their laser eyes red with frustration beneath hooded parkas. In the living-room, she sits slightly removed from Giulio. She's eating his mother's special cake, layered in vanilla and chocolate cream and soaked in vermouth. In time, she will herself learn to make it—and thick red sauce for the spaghetti. And the techniques for homemade sausage. And the rudiments of the Italian language. Only to leave it all behind on a wintry night, child in her arms, floating through the farmhouse roof. Is that when it happened? Pigeons come to life in the sudden warmth, flapping and cooing for attention. Hurling themselves against the chicken-wire mesh. Giulio's father slices potatoes and, after covering the pieces in salt and pepper, tosses them on to the sizzling stove top. The child Giulio reaches for one—unafraid of burning himself—and flips it into the thick air. It leaves a mark on his palm. Blasts him back into the greasy spoon.

"Listen, Pagan," he says, gripping, white-knuckled, the arm of the wheelchair. "Listen to me."

"What? What?"

"I think I have a solution to life."

"Why, what's the problem?"

"Just shut up and listen."

"All right. Okay. No need to get testy."

Giulio brings his face close to Pagan's. Places a hand on his friend's shoulder. Out of the corner of his eye, two figures pop out at last from a snow bank. They resume their jaunt down the street, merging as one as they cross the curtain into some other dimension.

"I was thinking," Giulio says, doing a double take as they disappear. "I was thinking: What if we're not here right now? What if we're at some other point in the past or future and only think we're here?"

"That's stupid," Pagan says with sudden anger and beginning to spin nervously. "Either we're here or we're nowhere, man. Absolutely fucking nowhere."

"Okay. So tell me then, Mr. Wise Ass Detective. Why do we keep losing things? Why do things we value have to be somewhere else? Or some time else? For example, sweet Pagan, where might your legs be? Tell me that. Where might your perfectly functioning legs be, eh?"

"Giulio, what the fuck are you talking about?" He's spinning faster and faster now. "Geez, I knew I should've never mentioned those butterflies. Those fucking butterflies are nothing but trouble."

"Could be. Could be. But you know what?"

"I'm almost afraid to ask." There is a pause. "What?"

"I'm just gonna sit here and wait for things to catch up. That's all."

"OK. You do that."

Pagan is spinning so fast, he's little more than a blur. He begins to rise, like a helicopter, the roar deafening.

"And if parts of you happen to come by, too, don't worry, Mr. Pagan man," Giulio shouts over the din. "I'll pick 'em up as well; I'll snare them with my fish-hook logic—they'll be a bargain!"

My poor Giulio.

Come on, now. I'm sure someone out there has a little arsenic to spare. Just a tiny little spoonful. Tucked away in a mouldy box beneath a mouldy stairwell. Left over from an Agatha Christie mystery, yes?

I could reach right in at the beginning, before it really gets started, and stir it into his coffee. Mix it in nicely so that he'd hardly notice the slightly bitter taste.

That would wipe away a lot of confusion, wouldn't it?

And I promise not to tell anyone who gave it to me.

Promise.

INTERMEZZO I: Moving on

I don't know. I just don't know.

There are times when I get an irresistible feeling to chuck it all away. To become a construction worker. Hammering, hammering. Or a demolitions expert. Pow! The satisfaction of a shower of rocks, granite jolted from its million-year sleep.

Sometimes, it just doesn't seem worth the effort. Here I am, filling reams of paper with funny little stick persons. I can make them cavort; I can make them cry; I can make them ask the reason why. But the thrill is gone. Know what I mean?

And, when I don't feel like chucking it all away, I want to poke the little buggers in the chest, rap a big knuckle against their fragile noggins, jam a finger down their throats. Or up any other available orifices. In other words, have some fun. But I know that won't do. An author has to be serious. Has to be responsible to his readers. And to his creations, I suppose.

Yes, but that doesn't mean he can't get involved, now does it? That doesn't mean he has to play it strictly by the book, does it?

I don't know. Sometimes, I just don't know.

Families, Friendlies, Familiars II

V. In the country

Tumultuously approaching 70, Giulio's mother still grips the knife as taut as a heart-string. And, because she wields it with the arrogance of a practiced killer, with the sure cockiness of a street fighter, death comes easy—and nary a squawk to be heard. Or at least it's as easy as it'll ever come. Knee pressed down on knobby chest, one hand stretching frantic head, it's all over in mere seconds (a primary example, I point out to Giulio, of matter over mind). Only the surprise of the whetstone-cold blade across a grizzled neck causes one final liquid-y befoulment. And the previous year's yellowing newspapers, stacked and put aside for just such an occasion, soak that up nicely, thank you very much. There is, of course, a continued spasmodic reaction for the next few minutes, legs kicking out, wings crack-flapping and head jerking from side to side. It's as if they have to fight for breathing space amid the half-dozen others already upside down in the bloody box that once (and I can vouch for this) did hold wine grapes. California wine grapes of various denominations. But everyone knows the kicking out of the legs, the wing-flapping, the jerking from side to side, the sudden lifting of the head, is nothing but the automatic firing of a very rudimentary nervous system. One last gasp before the retreat into the everlasting void: eyes half-hooded; cockscomb drained white; swollen tongue hanging, dangling, arrowhead-shaped, from the far edge of the beak.

Giulio's mother can do 60—give or take one or two either way—in a day, and with always the same precise and incisive slitting motion. Well, maybe, there is a slight slippage towards the end of the afternoon; maybe not quite as clean a cut or as enthusiastic a delivery of the knife-point as the morning's first entries. But that's understandable at her age and at a time (what with microwaves and multiple-setting automatic washing-machines) when she no longer has to shoulder the full brunt of the workload. Besides, she picks right up again after the coffee break and is always the first in position, urging the men to save their serious drinking for another day, for a more festive occasion. Her 70th birthday, for example, she'll say with a grin.

As Giulio sticks his arm into the cage to pull out the next in line, I'd like to think he contemplates the murky if unchanging rules of chance: What lottery causes me to take one and not the other? Is it just, is it fair, is it kosher that I always reach for the one closest to me, the one easiest to yank out without shredding legs or wings? For it wouldn't do to injure or damage the creatures before they are killed. That's a cardinal rule (not of chance this time but having to do with keeping the meat bloodless and tender, so that it looks good and cooks well on the barbecue). When you think about it, it doesn't really matter (there's that word again) which one he pulls out first, middle or last. There is no escape—only a few moments' grace, an opportunity to observe through beady eye the radical green of the grass, the earthworm-powdered soil between furry blades, the clack-whirring of a beetle's wings on lift off. Still, Giulio makes it a point on occasion (every half-hour or so, on average) to penetrate way back into the tight, practically airless cage, to snake around and ferret out the one looking the other way, head bulging through the bars of its imprisonment as if it all of a sudden "knows" the awful truth.

Yes, you! Giulio will say to himself. I'm talking to you (just as I'm talking to **you**). The one who seems to have achieved a measure, a modicum of self-consciousness, albeit a very restricted and conditional one. Let's just see what good it'll do you now, faced with the gleaming blade, the glint of honed steel, the sharp edge where not even Hobson's Choice is allowed to interfere.

Then, with one hand holding it upside down by the legs, and with the other folding the wings back so they can't flap loose, destructive despite their uselessness, he'll trap it one last time. And will place it on the killing block. And will press his knee against its chest—firmly but not so hard as to crush the breastbone. It is at this point that his mother will take hold of and stretch the creature's head as far as it'll go, talking to it the whole time (at least in the morning), imitating its cries, clucking and reprimanding it for not meeting its death in a more dignified way rather than spasming and splattering liquid shit within a three-meter radius.

And will slit. Once. Cleanly. To precisely the right depth, the standard width, thus avoiding both premature decapitation and undue stress. Especially undue stress.

Beneath its suddenly languid head, the dark pool of blood coagulates in a tin plate (which once did hold a homemade apple pie), dry-layered to indicate the pauses between kills. It's at this point that Giulio must really hang on for it bucks with the strength of the quasi-dead, flexes its muscles with the same sudden intensity as a mother who spots her child trapped beneath the wheels of a tractor.

When a half-dozen or so of the creatures have met their fate in this fashion, Giulio carries the box containing their corpses to the boiling pot. It is here that they are dunked and stripped of their grosser feathers; then moved on for further cleaning and carving. Occasionally, the wasps pick up the scent (or whatever it is they pick up) and come zooming in amid the still-hot entrails, the assembly-line that plucks, splits, guts and chops, thus completing the metamorphosis from ungainly living creature to enticing and tasty chunks of meat, appropriate for sizzling on the barbecue.

Giulio has—or rather had—or perhaps still has—a friend who's a vegetarian. It's at times like these, as he squats before the oily, seething, bubbling cauldron and yanks feathers from a scalded body, that he chooses to think of his friend. (It could be that "chooses" isn't the right word, but we'll let it go for now.) He thinks about the time his friend went storming out of his apartment—after calling the people in it dirty rotten stinking hypocrites because they were making noises of disgust during a documentary that showed, in graphic detail, the highly-automated slaughter of turkeys. (Look, ma, no hands— just a few electric prods and a finely-tuned flame thrower.) Giulio can't remember his friend's exact words (and I'm not going to make the effort) but they had to be something like: "How dare you make faces like that when all of you eat meat? When all of you take trips to the supermarket to buy it ready-packaged, the giblets left conveniently within?" ("The giblets left conveniently within" was without doubt a Giulio addition.) Another time, his friend walked out in the middle of a backyard party because Giulio was serving jumbo hot dogs, nicely roasted on one of those rotating spits that come as optional accessories for modern barbecues. It didn't help the situation much when one drunken guest (a lapsed metaphysician, no doubt) pointed out that hot dogs were, strictly speaking, not meat in an integral sense but rather collections of diverse parts from diverse places—a sort of Dr. Frankenstein monster creation delicacy made especially so as not to fall between the grill spacings (for those not blessed with optional barbecue spits).

Giulio didn't see his friend for several years after that final storming out—until he spotted him one afternoon sitting at the back of the bus, holding a woman's hand. Aha, Giulio had to have thought, he's tasted flesh after all—or is about to in short order. Following that, Giulio saw him several times along the same bus route, practically in the same seat. But he never stopped. Or waved. Or acknowledged his friend in any way. Giulio had always been like that, had always been the one not to make the first move (afraid, no doubt, of being rebuffed). And then, out of the blue, his friend started talking to him again, as if nothing had happened. He walked right up to Giulio one day and began a conversation that could have easily been a continuation of some previous one (for the record: it was). That woman on the bus turned out to be his new wife—and she was on the verge of pregnancy. Until recently, when he'd vanished once more, their two families had met occasionally, shared vegetarian dinners (on that his friend wouldn't compromise) and discussed computers. The last Giulio had heard, his friend had run afoul of some punk hoodlums who lived and worked in his neighbourhood (mostly break-ins and some protection rackets, according to my sources). Because he threatened to report them to the police after overhearing them plot a crime during a walk through the local park, they hinted his child and wife might be in danger—and made neck-slitting motions with their fingers to emphasize that fact. Obviously not professionals as they wouldn't have given themselves away so easily. Or for so little. But how was Giulio's friend to know the levels of professionalism in crime—unable even to eat what the rest of us took for granted and swallowed so easily? So he started to disguise himself each time he went out on the street: dark glasses, fedora, even a moustache and beard. Eventually, seeing enemies everywhere, he was forced to move out—practically in the middle of the night—leaving neither forwarding address nor telephone number.

Giulio stands up to give his aching legs a break, and, after checking it for drowned insects, takes a long swig of his now lukewarm beer. His mother, having finished with the killing, has washed her hands and proceeded to join the others in the dissecting. They are working quickly around the fixed cement table (a raised slab on two central posts, really), anxious to get everything done before dark makes the use of knives a danger. At the same time, they're laughing and telling jokes, keeping up a steady patter. Giulio's wife (it's still early in their marriage) poses for a picture—with a gutted chicken balanced on her head, the slit fitted neatly along her scalp. Giulio is very happy (or at least thinks he is—or I make him think he is—for it's the thinking that makes it so, is it not?). Already slightly drunk, he laughs from the gut and makes a comment about the Pope's bulbous nose just above her own pertly upturned one. He then walks over and picks up the scrap bucket filled with intestines, toe-nails, yellow clawpads, beaks, gizzards and the greenish contents of 60 stomachs (give or take one or two either way). This he hauls to the far end of the garden where a shallow hole has already been dug beneath a very healthy-looking plum tree, a plum tree nourished with the richest soil available. He empties the sloshy contents of the bucket into the hole, standing as far away as possible while doing so. Then he covers the steaming entrails—nothing now but leftover and very inert matter—with soft, extremely friable earth.

For a moment, the only sound is the angry buzzing of the fat, late-season flies as they rise in tandem from their hopeless breeding ground. And then settle again in the same spot. In exactly the same spot.

As if they've been genetically programmed.

Which, I guess, they have.

Which, *of course*, they have.

VI. Dans le métro

Naturally, when the word "subway" comes up in conversation, the first thing a person is apt to think of is suicide. That's a given—even for someone as good-natured and unsuicidal as Giulio. The determined blur across the windshield, forced into flying, striking the shatterproof pane at full impact. The sudden screech of brakes, smoke rising from the tracks. The unsuspecting passengers hurled forward in a perfect example—minus friction, of course—of Newton's First Law of Motion. Then, the inexplicable delays (inexplicable to most, in any case). The garbled announcements of electrical units out, emergency repair work to be done (it being a strict policy of the transit commission not to announce suicides). The growing anger and frustration of the commuters either jittery from a bone-crushing day at work or antsy to get down to their tasks before the time-clock alarms go off. The devil-may-care attitude of the teenagers who see it as an excuse for further making out where no parents are likely to intrude or attempt to pry them apart. The daring young children sticking their feet out as dangly as possible over the void of the tracks (to emphasize, no doubt, that it hadn't been merely a loss of balance, a slippage, that the act must have been an extremely deliberate one—if not in execution then at least in contemplation). Finally, the paste-faced look of the unlucky conductor as he or she is led out on shaky legs for some much-needed fresh air, followed by a dozen or so sessions of group therapy. All expenses paid.

But, as a matter of fact, Giulio likes taking the métro (which is a form of subway but on a completely different level of metaphor)—even in the midst of steel on steel, sudden applications of the macroscopic laws of motion and inexplicable delays. Maybe it's the cave-like descent, the live musical interludes ranging from lightest opera to heaviest metal, the rush of wind against his face as another train is sucked out of the station and into the tunnel, the coolness like that of a well-lit cellar in the midst of a tour featuring second-century catacombs, walls lined with bones rather than wine bottles. Or it might be something as simple as the fact most people let you alone, that no matter how crowded it gets, you always have your own space—unlike the bus, which has the opposite effect. Giulio has never given his reasons—at least not to me. Nor have I pressed him on it. Just that he likes it. Just that he prefers it to other modes of transportation. Public or otherwise.

But I could probably come up with a few reasons on my own. For one thing, judging from his actions, Giulio seems of the opinion the métro is the ideal place to read. Not only does he find it peaceful but the seating arrangement reduces the chance of eye contact with the other passengers. Eye contact is anathema no matter what the circumstances, a breach of conduct so fundamental and unforgivable Giulio wouldn't be surprised if it turned out to be the biggest factor in the suicides, if the eye contact and the leap that follows were not cause and effect. When he forgets his book (a very rare event in any case), he compensates by staring out through the side window. Now, staring out the window of a métro car is in no way comparable to staring out the window of a bus. For the obvious reason that a métro car runs on tracks through a tunnel, a very tight tunnel. Also, a métro car window becomes opaqued under tunnel conditions while a bus window remains clear and obvious. So what you see from a métro car window in a tunnel is mostly a reflection of the car itself—and yourself. Doubled back. And re-doubled. Two ghost trains running alongside the "real" one. On either side. It's a self-enclosed, self-feeding, umbilical cord world in all the important ways, all the ways that count—at least until you get to the station. And Giulio can well understand the ambivalence shown by the passengers. Some—those who believe in laying out detailed plans, who believe there is a ready-made world just waiting for them—might suffer from claustrophobia and suicidal tendencies, a fear of never seeing that world again; others—the anti-realists, the constructivists, those who put their faith in non-existent objects—might find it stimulating, a partial vindication of the way they feel on a full-time basis. As an experiment, the mass transit company once tried placing poster-ads along the walls of the tunnels. Giulio found it strange to suddenly fly by a bright blur of colours which no stretch of the imagination could unscramble—and which could be anything: from neo-Nazi propaganda to men performing fellatio on other men; from satanic messages to the true, unspeakable letters of God's name. Occasionally, however, the train would screech to a halt right in the middle of a tunnel (a disgruntled worker, no doubt, unable to hold out till the weekend after suddenly realizing that the code before him *did* make sense—but had nothing to say to him). And then, in this abortion of velocity, this accelerated deceleration, the colours would revert to ordinary, vapid poster-ads, with ordinary, vapid sales pitches. So, it was best not to forget your book—even after the transit company gave up on the subliminal posters (connected, I would imagine, to a commissioned study that showed they hadn't helped in the least to lower the suicide rate—and may have, in fact, contributed).

Among the few other annoyances (distractions, perhaps, is a better word in this case) in the métro are the occasional pan-handlers, betting that they can earn somewhat more than the price of the ticket it cost them to get through the turnstiles. Most of these people are extremely polite and meek, holding out their hands all-atremble and bending over towards you with the studied diffidence and tilted-head scorn of an old-style man-servant. Or a barnyard rooster. Then, whispering for a dime, a quarter, anything to buy a coffee. Giulio finds himself sweating whenever one of these comes near him, usually preceded by an odour like that of organic material left first in the rain for several days and then allowed to dry up again under a merciless sun. Using the fingers of his one free hand (holding the book tightly with the other), he searches through the coins in his pocket, feeling for the exact ones he wants without having to take them all out for the world to see—and thus able to judge his charity. Or better still, he keeps several coins in a separate pocket. That way, the pan-handlers don't get the opportunity to approach too close (risking nausea) before he fends them off with his mute offering.

Not all the pan-handlers, however, are this meek. One, in particular, a thick-set, florid-faced man with a permanent scowl, is so aggressive Giulio's surprised he hasn't yet been escorted away by the ever-vigilant métro security, armed with the latest billy club technology and an unbeatable air of command. This pan-handler likes to push his pimply face right up against a potential donor and then to whine at the top of his voice: "Fifty ce...e...e...nts." He does this to every person on the métro platform, working one side and then the other, becoming more and more belligerent till he wanders off, swearing in exactly the same whining tone of voice: "Fuck y...o...o...o...u." And it doesn't matter if he receives a contribution or not, if it's a dime or a dollar. He offers no "Thank you" or "God bless" under any conditions, only that favourite Anglo-Saxon crudity. Giulio has never given this man a single cent. Not because of his attitude—Giulio actually appreciates it after so much meekness, so much kowtowing—but because he once spotted a monthly transit pass in the man's trembling hand.

But Giulio obviously hasn't worked this through, has on this occasion let his thinking cloud his emotions. The man may have found the pass; it may have been a gift from a commuter who'd recently purchased a car; it may have been the previous month's pass and thereby useless except as a collector's item for someone who pins such objects on the wall like butterflies. Despite this, and fully realizing what a sympathetic character Giulio is, my advice to him would still be: Stand on principle. Don't dip into your special pocket the next time he shouts his whining demand within centimetres of your face. Let him know you disapprove even if there's nothing to disapprove of. Giulio, of course, as soon as he reads this (and he reads everything I place in his path), will break into one of his famous sweats—and over-compensate the moment he runs into that moaning "Fifty c...e....n...t...s! Fuck y...o...o...o...u!"

There is one other person who can disrupt Giulio's quiet sojourning beneath the city. Well, he isn't the only one actually of his kind. There are graduates from the Oral Swaggart Correspondence College of Christian Advocacy, for example, young adults mostly with name tags on their lapels, who sometimes come up to him and start a conversation without even the benefit of eye contact: "Hi, I'm Barry from Cleveland, Ohio. The U.S. of A. I've been sent up here as part of my missionary training in foreign countries. I can't speak the native language yet but I'm learning real fast. Très fast. I see you're reading—and in a language I understand. That's very fine—to read, that is. The word is important to all of us, isn't it? What are you reading?" He leans over to look at the cover. "Ah, Albert Einstein Meets Godzilla. Don't know it—but have you tried reading these instead?" And Giulio would shake his head, smile benignly and go back to the book before him, to the point where a renegade, glint-eyed Einstein tries to explain to Godzilla how to use the special theory of relativity to more effectively raze a city. And, eventually, after standing there for a few awkward moments, inspirational material in hand, the Jimmy Ted Swaggart or Garner Roberts or Oral Armstrong trainee would get the hint.

But this man is definitely special. For one thing, he's dressed completely in black: from his spotless, polished shoes to his Marks & Spencer turtle-neck sweater with the discreet crocodile logo. Adding to the effect is the fact the man himself is what's popularly called black, though creased brown would be a better description. This man has taken upon himself the task of marching up and down the métro cars, waving a worn, discoloured, sweat-stained bible in his hand as he shouts imprecations and blessings as loudly as possible above the sound of screeching brakes: "*Nous sommes tous sur un voyage! Un très long voyage! Les noirs, les blancs, les jaunes! Et c'est le bon Dieu notre guide! Notre conducteur. La deuxième classe n'existe pas sur ce voyage!*" Occasionally, and seemingly at random, he likes to single out one particular passenger in the car. Then he recites the entire speech to that person—right up in his or her face. If the potential convert moves, as many are wont to do after several minutes of being so mercilessly harangued, he simply trails along behind them, still reciting, still waving the bible. Giulio was chosen once for that singular treatment. Fortunately, it was one of the times that he hadn't forgotten his book and he was able to weather the storm with only a few beads of sweat breaking out on his forehead. But, more importantly, without having to make eye contact. Still, in his irritation, Giulio found himself thinking: I look forward to the day when the salvation-shouting preacher and the swearing-shouting pan-handler end up in the same métro car.

(That day does come about and with interesting and unexpected results—but I make sure Giulio isn't there to witness it. It would be too much for him to bear.)

A final hint: Giulio, if you really insist on killing yourself in the métro, I would advise you to stand as close as possible to the mouth of the tunnel, to where it breaks open into the grand vault of the station itself. Pressed against the wall if you can manage it without arousing undue suspicion from the ever-vigilant métro security. Pretend an interest in layered graffiti, in the composition of the concrete, in the progress of a wasp that has had the misfortune of following the wrong scent. Whatever. At that point, the incoming train hasn't had time to slow down much and is still travelling at a reasonable clip. Even more important, the conductor can't really see you behind that slightly pulsing wall, can't really make you out until it's too late. The one thing you don't want is for him or her to hit the brakes before hitting your body. And, as you fly across that friendless space, smile if you remember. Or wave. It'll ease the trauma—at least on any conductor that I'd select.

(Okay, okay. Since you so insist on knowing, since you're not above using emotional blackmail to get an answer, here it is: There is a powerful, métro-shattering explosion when the pan-handler and the preacher meet. And out of that explosion there emerges ... Adolf Hitler ... Buddha ... Gandhi ... Everyman ... Louis Riel ... another Giulio ... and another. . . .)

Satisfied?

Thought not.

VII. And the attendance of weddings: a dialogue

ME: Anyone who has ever accepted an invitation to an Italian wedding knows what it's like: the grandparents having group sex in the washroom; the knives and forks sticking pell-mell out of the guests' backs; the bride gutted—split from crotch to throat—with a gold-plated can opener; the father-in-law fondling the youngest and fairest of the flower girls; the wine turned into water; the bridegroom and the best man. . . .

GIULIO: (*with more than a hint of indignation*): Wait a minute. Wait just a fucking minute. What are you saying? Is this some sort of joke? If so, I don't think it's all that funny. And the Anti-Defamation League won't, either. What you're describing certainly doesn't sound like any wedding I've ever attended. And I've been to dozens, believe me. Take my third cousin's, for instance, on my mother's side. Now, *that* was a classic Italian wedding. It had everything: from the solemnity of the Nuptial Mass to the plates heaped high with lobster tails and steak; from the first father-daughter waltz to the last falling-down-drunk *Tarantella*; from the group photo on the church steps to the video camera sweeping majestically, if somewhat erratically, across the reception hall. I know, I know. Trite shit. Mundane. But that's the kind of stuff that makes for memories. And, in the end, what else have we got, really?

ME: Giulio is right, of course. It's just that we all see those memories from different perspectives, don't we? Twist them with our own peculiar prism. Besides, it wouldn't be fair for me to rely on one third cousin's wedding—or even a bundle of such weddings—for my assumptions.

And, if I did, there's no guarantee it would lead to the same conclusion as Giulio's. In fact, I'm positive it wouldn't—as no adding of one assumption to another guarantees anything but the sum of those assumptions. And that's not what I'm looking for. It's the idea itself of "Italian Wedding" that fascinates me: that unholy bubbling and seething below the smooth, well-oiled surface—the affirmation of the not-quite-civilized and the untamed, of barter and property exchange. In my version of that idea, there are grandparents who perform acrobatic sex acts against washroom sinks and toilet bowls, their bifocals askew, their false teeth clattering to the marble floor, rheumatoid hands grasping at depleted, blue-veined breasts, arthritic fingers undoing rusted zippers, fuse-jointed hips wrapped around discoloured, fatally bruised thighs. They are giving each other blow jobs, performing fellatio and cunnilingus while standing on their heads, pyramid-screwing until they're panting and clutching at their pacemakers—each trying to outdo the other in a frenzy of aspic flesh and quivering jelly. And, all the while, the ashen, gaunt-faced washroom attendant keeps looking at his over-sized time-piece, bored out of his mind, just itching for the moment when he can say: "That's it! Tick tock! Time's up, ladies and gentlemen." And then everything can stop dead. In its tracks.

GIULIO: I see. A symbolism. Puppet characters lewd-dancing to your vicarious bidding, your finger-snapping. Their genitals increasing and decreasing in size according to your whim. The last priapic remnants of a bacchanalia best forgotten. Evoe! and all that. But, let me tell you, the grandparents at my third cousin's wedding are nothing of the sort. Peasants with a far-away look in their eyes (attributable mostly to the loss of retinal pigmentation), they would be able to make no sense of your symbolism. It would be lost on them. They wouldn't even understand the words you're using to describe their actions, to catalogue their perversions. This they understand: The

bride's grandfather is tight with his money and parts
his hair to the right. He likes to complain about his
homemade wine, claiming it doesn't match up to yours.
Occasionally, he still takes a trip to the pool hall around
the corner. The bridegroom's grandmother has the cutest
and fluffiest silver hair—a wig actually. She smiles a lot—
especially when the knives and forks strike the plates.
She herself joins in when she can, the natural tremor in
her movements enough to set the plates a-ringing with a
tinkle both romantic and urgent.

ME: Ah, the knives and forks, the ever-present knives and
forks. Now I remember. Guided by motherhood,
righteousness, neighbourly concern, they fly across the
wide, crystal-chandeliered hall, lodging in the most
convenient, the least protected, the fleshiest of backs.
Very discriminating in their stabbing, aren't they?
Motherhood stands up and starts to hurl: *Look at that
Mrs. Cippencullo. How, in her condition, can she be so
brazen as to wear a yellow dress? Wasn't her son only
yesterday released from the loony bin? Just a day pass, you
say. So he could attend the wedding, right?* Righteousness
spins a knife, aims for the bull's-eye: *Hey, Affamate.
How's the import-export business going? Good, good. No
problem with the funny white stuff the police found in the
hollowed-out cores of your statues? Naw, didn't think so.*
Finally, there's the all-important neighbourly concern.
Where would Italian weddings be without neighbourly
concern? Mr. Lazzaronne is writhing in the corner, the
knives and forks sticking out of him in every direction.
Rumours are he's dying, just wasting away. No, his wife
is dying, stomach swelling from the cancer. No, he's
been cuckolded by the milkman who has his own way of
churning the butter—if you know what I mean. No, he's
having an affair with his mono-browed Sicilian secretary.
No, it's a matter of incest. No, no, no. You've all got it
wrong. Investigators have discovered Mr. Lazzaronne
collaborated with the Fascists. Turned in his own father
for the castor oil cure—even though he was only four at

the time. But neighbourly concern won't allow this to go on. One by one, with just the right touch of motherhood and righteousness, it pulls the knives and forks out of the unfortunate Mr. Lazzaronne. Starting with the carving blade in the dead centre of his back, the one he probably stuck in himself.

GIULIO: More symbolism. Don't you ever get tired of it? Why don't you do the people once in a while? The real people, I mean. Have trouble with them, eh? Here. Here's the group photo, taken right after the Mass. I know, I know. You're going to tell me they got married under a canopy that features Mussolini and his horse quite prominently.

ASIDE: Boy, Giulio's getting very good at this—that's exactly what I was going to bring up.

GIULIO: But I don't care. It's the group photo I'm talking about. There must be a hundred people in that photo, packed in tight, shoulder to shoulder, on the various levels of the church steps. The bride and groom are at the very bottom, at the very centre of the very bottom. That's me in the corner, the one with the shades. I know each one of those approximately one hundred people. With a little prompting, I can name them for you. Well, most of them anyway. They all come from the same village in Italy. Or from a neighbouring village by way of marriage. Agio— close exchange of the foreign kind, I guess you could call it. They all crossed the ocean—at first by ship, then by plane. They all came to the same city on the other side of the ocean—to seek their fortune, as the saying goes. Yet they're individuals, flesh-and-blood—not symbols. Or lumps you can shape into your own crazed image. I think you should know that. It's important for me that you know that. It makes me angry when you treat them like symbols, when you impose your own vision on them. No matter how valid that might be. Since that photo was taken, several have met with untimely ends. One was hit by a car; the other found a spot on her lungs. But I have the photo—and the photo reminds me that, at some point in the evening, I danced wildly with Lung Spot, spinning until the rest of the room vanished in a wash of fermenting colours. Later, I traded second-rate jokes with Car Crash in the washroom—jokes that I've long since forgotten, but which made me laugh like a fool at the time. All I ask now is that you respect their memories. Is that so hard? So much to ask?

ME: Giulio, Giulio. Though not a complete innocent, you've always had a tendency to let your heart do the thinking. Definitely a character defect that (for the sake of internal logic) I've left untouched. But, now that you've managed to stir this particular emotional pot, this slick-oiled cauldron, where do we go from here? It's all very well to raise the spectre of family attachment, of beatific bonding and bliss-laden vows. But let's get real, shall we? The bride is property. The men line up to have a crack at her, their fish-hook penises hoping to snare her insides, the essentials she's tried to keep back all these years. Now, because the price is right, she has to give them up—in front of all those smiling faces. And she herself has to smile about it, to keep up appearances for the sake of the ultra-modern tiled and terrazzoed kitchen she'll inherit. Come on, I dare you to open that bathroom door. Surprise! Isn't that someone's father-in-law diddling the youngest and fairest flower girl? Hey, diddle, diddle, playing with the cat's fiddle. And, slipping out the back, didn't I see the bridegroom running away with the best man, hand-in-hand and one powdery spoon between them? Okay, so I was wrong about the wine being turned into water. But I think I can be forgiven for that one little piece of hyperbole. Can't I, Giulio? Come on, what do you say? Tell me you forgive me. Your forgiveness is worth so much to me.

GIULIO (*with more than a hint of anger*): It's your call. Do as you wish. After all, nothing I've ever said before has had the slightest effect on you.

ME: That's not true! And a low blow to boot. But we'll let it go for now. Right now, all I want from you is for you to say the words: "I forgive you."

GIULIO: (*anxious*): Just leave me with my memories. That's all I
　　　　　ask—all I care about.

ME　　 (*coyly*): Giulio, I haven't heard those magic words yet. You
　　　　　know as well as I do no miracles can take place without
　　　　　those words—not even in the most unlikely of tales.

GIULIO: Alright, alright. I'll forgive you if you leave my memories
　　　　　intact. I want those snapshots and faded wedding photos
　　　　　burnt forever into my neurons.

ME:　　 Let's see now. Hmmm, let's see if I've got this straight.
　　　　　Your forgiveness for a guarantee of identity. Hmmm.
　　　　　Sure, why not. Sounds like a good deal to me.

GIULIO: Okay, then. I forgive you. Or maybe I should put the
　　　　　whole thing in quotes: "I forgive you."

ME:　　 Good. Very good. Now, where were we? What exactly am I
　　　　　being forgiven for?

GIULIO: For . . . for weddings . . . no . . . for . . . Shit! I don't know.
　　　　　(Here, there's an image of Giulio racking his brains. Or
　　　　　scratching his head, at least, as brain-racking is such a
　　　　　difficult image to portray properly). I can't remember.
　　　　　Godammit. What have you done to me? What have you
　　　　　done to me now?

ME　　 (*with undisguised derision*): Giulio, you're such a sap.
　　　　　Look at you. All curled up like a small child amid the
　　　　　detritus of yet one more wedding. Or is it a funeral? You
　　　　　still haven't realized how many lies I've told, am telling,
　　　　　and have yet to tell—but only as a way to get to the truth,
　　　　　of course. You understand that much, don't you? I'm sure
　　　　　you do. (I'm sure he does).

VIII. He visits a friend

It's May 31st, 1987. Well, not really. But I make it so. President Reagan is giving a speech.

What does this have to do with Giulio, you ask?

Well, Giulio thinks that all deaths are pretty much alike. In one scenario, it's a pleasant late-spring day and a jolly, curly-haired, ru-by-faced God (one of my better guises) is standing on a street-corner picking out possible victims at random as they stroll by—a variation on the "I got you, babe" theme. It's most fun to select the ones who consider themselves to be in the best of health—or sun-tanned and well-dressed, seemingly without a care in the world and with a brilliant, bright, glowing, positively incandescent future. In another, a hand snakes into a cage (office, condo, love nest) and someone says: "Sssh!" and the lights go out. Snap. In a third, the middle of the night grabs you by the throat and won't let go—not even when the alarm clock rings with news of your salvation.

Giulio may have these very vivid imaginings of death: his own death, his parents' deaths, the deaths of acquaintances and total strangers. But the bodies have always been interchangeable—almost superimposed on one another. A blur of faces and hair-lines and mummified smiles too late getting the respect they have so loudly clamoured for while alive. So that doesn't help much. Nor do the long-distance deaths announced by misspelled telegrams or crack-ling phone calls from across the ocean. From "The Old Country".

That's why I decide it's time for him to visit his friend. Much against his will, I must point out. In fact, I practically have to drag him there, kicking and screaming, an invisible hand reaching in and pulling him by the scruff of the neck. He keeps coming up with all kinds of excuses: the neighbourhood makes him queasy with all its marble steps, red Camaros and bird-bath statues; the family hasn't sent him an invitation; his friend doesn't really want to see him; he lost the directions the last time he emptied out his pockets.

And he tries to turn back several times before I finally force him to ring the doorbell—pushing his clenched fist against it after a battle of wills he knows he'll lose. I remember him thinking (having him think): "Jeez, it still sounds the lively tune of a *Tarantella Siciliana*. Wouldn't a few notes from a funeral march—Debussy or one of those classical sourpusses—be more appropriate under the circumstances? Even a neutral 'ding-dong' would be acceptable if the re-programming instructions proved too much for the simple peasant mind. On the other hand, perhaps they did change it once and now have changed it back—because things have improved to this extent, at least. Yeah, that's it. Things have definitely improved—and it's going to be Bob Dylan's *A Hard Rain's A Gonna Fall* next, my friend's all time favourite."

Wishful thinking. The moment Giulio steps into the house, he knows nothing has improved, that, if anything, the slide has been greased, that the cusp geometry of the to-be-expected unexpected reigns supreme. A figure draped from head-to-toe in black—his friend's mother—flits by, all hunched over. She turns towards him for a moment, charcoal-eyed, unrecognizable and unrecognizing—and then vanishes into one of the side rooms. There, he can hear her beating her head against the wall: so rhythmically you could, as the expression goes, set your watch by it. In the interior designer kitchen, his friend's father sits, squat and unshaven, in his underwear, one hand on a gallon of homemade red, the other rubbing a glass back and forth across the terrazzo tabletop. (His own workmanship, I should point out). The latest-model halogen track-lighting aims a violet spotlight directly on the father's balding head, a discoloration that's clownish in its effect. But the man himself isn't laughing and doesn't bother looking up when he hears Giulio walking past. Nor does he make the effort to offer him a glass of the homemade—under normal circumstances an unforgivable discourtesy.

It's his friend's sister who leads him into the invalid's room, a room he hasn't entered in years. But Giulio still has vivid memories of it from their shared childhood, a time when they would use any excuse to sleep over, lying there poking and prodding each other and giggling until the sun itself intruded on their revelry. At first he can't see him and it seems that little has changed, that it's an early summer morning and school's out and the air is heady with lilac scent and the baseball gloves pop with studied languorousness. (In deference to Giulio's pronounced sensibilities, I've arranged for the curtains to be drawn, the lights dimmed, his friend with his face to the wall). But then, sighing, the friend turns in the bed. Giulio takes one step back—a reaction he can't help even while realizing he's doing it. Though knowing that doesn't lessen his guilt in having done it. Giulio's second reaction is: "This isn't my friend. No way. He's not the happy-go-lucky, full-of-mischief kid I went to high school with. He's not the one with whom I shared so many mortadella and provolone sandwiches, so many wrestling matches, so many hell-bent two-for-one bike rides from the top of the mountain to the dangerous unpatrolled edges of the artificial lake."

And he knows that is even worse than the first reaction. (And he knows that I know). For there is absolutely no doubt as to the identity of the man lying before him. His friend calls out his name and pats the bed. Giulio goes through numerous calculations (distances? possibilities? projections?) before finally sitting down on the edge. It is then that he notices the luminous quality of his friend's eyes, beautiful, unnaturally large, almost bulbous and bulging like that of a stereotypical friendly alien—in direct contrast to the scarred and sunken cheeks, the open sores about the lips, the purplish splotches across the temple and forehead. Giulio tries not to flinch when his friend takes his hand and gives it a gentle squeeze. It feels as if he were being touched by a butterfly, by one of those nymphs left behind when an insect undergoes metamorphosis (an incomplete metamorphosis, in this case, I hasten to point out to Giulio who isn't really listening).

Then, without ceremony, his friend begins to speak. He tells Giulio everything he doesn't want to hear, the secrets he in no way wants to know: how he will be dead within weeks, how all treatments have been exhausted, how each day he manages less and less, how the parts of his body are shutting down one by one, how the coma awaits him like a final blessing, the end-game called relief. But that's nothing compared to the recital of psychic pain Giulio has to endure. It turns out his friend's parents won't accept—or continually deny in the face of hard evidence—what has been happening. At first, they fixate (that's the friend's word) on the idea he has cancer.

Leukemia. Some rare blood disorder. One of those new super-duper hanta-viruses or something. All it needs is the proper doctor to conduct the proper diagnosis. Followed by the proper treatment and cure. When they can no longer hold onto that, when he confronts them head on and tells them he is dying from AIDS-related complications, they retreat to a different silence. Now, it's the incalculable perils of living in a big bad city; the awful danger of using communal toilets; the terrible cruelty of their son being picked out randomly for senseless destruction by a cruel, uncaring God. (That's a little unfair. Granted I'm not always so ruby-faced and jolly—but "cruel" and "uncaring"?). And each has shrunk away to their own private world. What will the neighbours say? How can we face up to our relatives? Who'll support us in our old age? Why us? Why us? Why us? He hasn't bothered telling them he is gay. That would be an utter and complete waste of breath. They wouldn't believe him, no matter how many character witnesses and lovers he calls in. He was handsome, athletic, outgoing, a fine catch for any of the signorinas who had, until a few years back, come knocking regularly on their side door. Neither of his parents have approached him since the illness made itself manifest. Nor have they hugged him or offered consolation of any kind. Not that they wouldn't like to—they just don't know how. Instead, they do their crying privately, weeping for a son who will never fulfill that early promise, the map they laid out for him as far back as the day they baptized him. And his father has spent a lifetime slaving away for him, hauling bricks up the sides of buildings 12 hours a day, six days a week, so they could afford this ritzy house in this ritzy neighbourhood. He has denied himself everything, the least pleasure. And his mother has abandoned her sacred duties as a housewife to do piecework at a sweat shop, slowly going blind in the dim light, feeling her pricked and bruised fingers creaking to a halt. And for what? Ah, misfortune follows us around; bad luck sticks to us; the mal'occhio crossed the ocean with us and has re-doubled its strength in this accursed land, this land where disease can rear up from the nearest toilet bowl.

His friend stops talking and lies back on the pillow, at the same time releasing Giulio's hand. Giulio can now hear the sister sobbing in one of the dark corners of the room. He feels sticky all over. He's about to say something when his friend lifts his head and stops him with his hand: I know. You're going to ask me why I don't go to a hospital or a hospice to die. At least, there I would have professional nurses and care-givers, right? Giulio nods. But you see, this is my family. Asp that I am, I want to die snug in the bosom of my family. They may spurn me but I can't spurn them. I've spent my life trying to win their love. Now, I think I might finally be able to do it.

Giulio feels the cold air as he walks back out through the house, the sweat drying on his body, the steam rising from his scalp. The last thing his friend had asked was that Giulio hug him. Giulio's hands had traced the wasted, bony ridges of his spinal cord, the individual ribs unravelling to leave the chest cavity defenceless. It was then that he'd finally understood the thin membrane that separated them—the brazenly alive and the for-all-practical-purposes dead. Both approximations of some other condition. (But I'm not at liberty to come right out and tell Giulio what that other condition might be. I'll leave that for some later occasion. Or I might leave it for him to figure out).

Nor do I allow him to look back once he has stepped outside. That's strictly verboten. For, if he were to look back, he would surely notice the entire family—mother, father, sister, brother—standing at the front window. They are standing at the picture window, arm in arm, smiling. They are standing at the interior design picture window, arm in arm, smiling—and proud of themselves. So very proud of themselves.

And who's that behind them, urging them to take a well-deserved bow for the performance of a lifetime? Why, yours truly, of course. As jolly, curly-haired, and ruby-faced as ever.

Beside me? Oh, that's just the President. Having finished his speech, he thought he'd also pay Giulio's friend a visit.

IX. He goes to school

Giulio considers himself an independent-minded and free-thinking individual. (That's always within the confines and definition, of course, of the sympathetic character. Couldn't have him suddenly and without warning go berserk, Uzi in hand, in an Israeli shopping mall, now could I? I could, however, have him suddenly and without warning fall madly in love—with a PLO intellectual. Or decide to go for his driving licence—even if it's a little late in his life for that.) In other words, within the confines of the sympathetic character, I allow him to do pretty much as he pleases when he pleases—as long as he follows through on those choices.

For example, he often disagrees with the direction I've chosen for a particular story—sometimes with a healthy amount of vehemence. I always let him have his say in these matters—even if I've decided beforehand that nothing will change my mind, even if I already know each and every argument before he spells them out. I feel it's important for him to have his own opinions and to work those opinions out in a manner that is both logical and passionate. It's all part of creating a solid, fully-rounded character, a personage that's believable on some level or other, even if he risks seeming irrational—or simply hard-headed—from the outside.

Giulio can also be quite quirky. There was the time he got it into his head to hike the length of the city-island on which he lived (and still does as a matter of fact): from one bridge tip to the other. All 100 or so kilometres of it, armed with nothing but a doubly-insulated pup tent and a sleeping bag. Not in the summer, mind you, but in the midst of a howling winter storm. It's a two-day affair at the best of times and just about impossible under Arctic conditions—as some of his friends tried to point out to him. But Giulio listens only to his own counsel—and the more outlandish the task the more stubborn he becomes when facing opposition. So there he was, taking the métro to the end of the line, then transferring to a taxi for the final ride to his starting point on the Eastern tip of the island. Four hours of snow-shoeing and ten kilometres into the trek, he decided he wasn't so sure anymore. At the twenty-five kilometre mark, he was definitely ready to pack it in—especially since he found himself close to his own neighbourhood (a hot meal; a glass or two of homemade; worn, friendly slippers; the inviting glow of his favourite *National Geographic* program—or an old-style sitcom where the *pater familias* knows best). But, for the sake of freedom and several other similar principles which he professes to hold so dear, I wouldn't allow him to back out at that point. No sir. I put my foot down and forced him to do the same with his—over and over again. Well, let me tell you, by the time he reached the far Western end of the island (as the sun was going down on a landscape that resembled nothing so much as the one on Pluto), he realized exactly what it meant to be free. And what it meant to have frostbite on most of his outer extremities. (Are there "inner" extremities? I suppose it's possible.) To this day, he has no memory of how he managed, with fingers like brittle breadsticks, to set up the tent that first night—or why he was still alive the following morning even though the temperature had dropped to minus 30 (not to mention the wind chill factor, the ever-present wind chill factor).

But, as much as I like to give Giulio a long leash, there are certain things over which I insist on retaining complete and absolute control—and one of those is his dream-state. The way I see it, the dream-state is far too important to leave to chance—or to what some call free choice, that peculiar commodity characters seem to cherish so highly. Besides, it's a wonderful opportunity to experiment (mix and match is what I call it in my more flippant moments). So I make it a point never to let Giulio know beforehand what his subconscious will conjure up for any particular night. Or rather what I, through his subconscious, have in store for him.

Here's a sample: Giulio is sitting on the lower slopes of a nondescript cliff, staring out at a full moon and listening to the waves beat against crepuscular rocks. It is late evening and the sea beneath him sparkles with silver needles. Tingling and delightful. For some reason (ha, ha), he decides he'd like to go for a skinny dip. Right now. At this very moment. Without delay. Immediately. The urge is beyond his control. So he removes his clothes and places them neatly on the rock face. Then, he stands for a moment stock still, unmoving. The moon silhouettes him: the stick-thin, praying-mantis limbs, the slightly-protruding belly, the less-than-barrel chest, the limp retreating penis with its tiny drop of ambient fluid. He calls out some words of self-encouragement and, taking a running leap, plunges off the cliff. Only to discover that the silver flashes in the sea aren't at all the reflections of moonbeams on choppy water. Not at all romantic moonbeam reflections. But rather billions upon billions of ravenous beetle grubs, all looking up greedily, all clacking their mandibles in anticipation, all anxious to reduce Giulio's body to shiny, polished, gleaming bone in a matter of seconds. And only when the first grub slithers through his eye socket, arching up towards the silvery moon (more beetle grubs?), do I allow him to wake. Soaked in sweat and checking to make sure his eyeballs are still there.

It is along the same vein that Giulio finds himself wandering once again the hallowed halls of his old high school. And he thinks: This can't be. This isn't possible. They turned the school into a refugee retraining centre not long after I graduated, a place where they take the raw materials that wash up on our promised-land shores and convert them into model citizens, complete with glowing faces, health-care teeth and tiny, starch-injected flags. But, despite the fact he's right (and knows he's right), the thought doesn't help. For all intents and purposes, Giulio *is* walking along the school corridor (as he had walked towards a plum tree, down a métro escalator, into a darkened room, across a barren wintry landscape). Because it happens to be a dream doesn't make it any less real—only more unpredictable.

At the end of the corridor, all green and gold, is his classroom, so normal and unchanged down through the years. In fact, if Giulio were to look closely enough he might still see the spot on the ceiling where the cafeteria cup-cake had once hung suspended for a good five minutes—before coming back down with a splat right in the midst of an explanation on The Passive Periphrastic Conjugation. Or the scuff marks of eternal shuffling, day in and day out, back and forth, with no sign it would ever come to an end. Or the exact way the sunlight filtered in at 2:45 p.m. on beams of tired dust, carrying with them the extremely-contagious yawning fever. But that's all ground. (Even though in some dreams it can easily become figure with desks flapping their wings and flying off; books flinging themselves into passionate argument; chalk and other school supplies suddenly staging a wild-cat strike; the image of the Virgin Mary above the teacher's head doing a slow strip-tease—and duplicated in every classroom as little boys with suddenly satyric proportions masturbate beneath their desks).

It's at this point, as Giulio walks into the classroom, that some decisions have to be made: Is this the dream where Giulio finds himself the last English-speaking person in the entire city? And he has returned to the school one final time to pick up pieces of his past, the indelibly-inked proof of his memories, stamped and legalized papers that will give him permission to continue speaking his adopted language? Only to discover that it really has been converted into a refugee retraining centre after all—and the desks are occupied by row on row of eager, smiling (glowing) faces, waving their little erectile flags, anxious to please, to know the answers before the questions are even asked? And they've all been given his identity, they've all been told they can be Giulio because Giulio has abandoned whatever claim he ever had to himself, has recited the oath of allegiance backwards once too often? Now, without warning, the perfect smiles turn to frowns, literally flip upside-down. The refugees have realized there are only a certain number of citizenships to go around—and definitely not enough for all of them. They are fighting over scraps of his identity, performing a radical translation, picking up the shredded bits. Giulio finds himself shrinking, in danger of being trodden underfoot. Giant-sized stamp pads are trying to eradicate him, trying to make him part of an official seal. And, for some reason, he suddenly thinks of borders being created where there were none before; armed guards springing up to make sure those leaving don't take anything of value with them (perhaps not even their family jewels); men in double-breasted suits and gold buttons knocking on his door with repossession notices: You've been found unfit to be a property owner under the Purity Law Regulations. As of today, this house belongs to a family whose worthiness is magnificently reflected in its name and 300-year pedigree—and whose bones just happen to be buried in the deepest corner of the basement. Right above those of the original squatters who never bothered with such legalities.

That's guaranteed to get poor Giulio in a sweat, to send him scurrying in the middle of the night for his birth certificate, his citizenship papers, his school eligibility documents, his Deed of Sale, the all-important Deed of Sale. Not to mention the Servitudes that allow him to legally get along with his neighbours. And, still not fully awake, he gathers the credentials around him, re-assures himself with their texture and solidity by rubbing them over his body, and faxes copies to various addresses around the country. There, now he feels better, more secure. Now, he can go back to sleep. If he doesn't make it out, if he doesn't make it past the rubber stamp, past the double-breasted suits, past the hermetically-sealed borders, at least he won't be left without an identity. Even if he himself won't know what that identity is.

Or is it the dream in which he's sexually assaulted by one of his teachers? A dream of retro-history that features the Little Brothers in Christ (or Christ's Brothers or some such similar disorder) and all the questions that weren't asked at the time but which of late have become so relevant and so necessary? Suddenly, there's no one else around. The other students have all vanished, casually seated one moment and gone the next. Giulio is making his way through the school, tip-toeing to prevent echoes, to stay anger and the sound of sour-stenched leather tapping against soutaned thigh. Ah, there it is: the door. He's almost out, almost ready for the daily trek home. But, when he comes to the exit, the cut-out in the wall through which he's escaped for as long as he can remember, it's not to be found in its rightful place. It has become a bricked-up barrier from which the faces of his fellow students shine in unnatural happiness, with rosy-cheeked wonder. He turns back, cultivating a nonchalant air—not yet too disturbed, not yet too concerned. Perhaps the girls' entrance is available. Even though he normally needs a special pass, he could always get through under extraordinary circumstances: illness, a death in the family, an inability to find the boys' entrance. It's just a matter of explaining. Besides, he doesn't really want to go into the forbidden zone of the girls' side. Not at all. He just needs to use that entrance to get outside, to fly down the steps, to arrive at the point where the bus still waits with rumbling impatience to take him home. But no. Explanation won't be possible on this occasion. The passageway connecting the two sides of the school is not only locked, barred and bolted. It's actually soldered shut, the lead still hissing and glowing silver as it cools. And, through the plate-glass, he can see one of the sister-executioners standing guard at the far end: black-hooded, legs apart, with muscles that ripple like waves in her spandex pants and holding a two-edged axe across her pointed breasts. Giulio spins and turns back. The doors to the classrooms close one by one as he goes by, leaving him no choice. And, just to make sure, a giant hand reaches in (hello there) and tilts the entire school, toppling him over. Giulio slides across the gleaming, newly-waxed linoleum floor, his nails scratching, scrambling, clutching in vain for some kind of hold. No amount of twisting and turning can save him though. Or screaming for that matter. There's only one room left that's still open, at the far end of the corridor, yawning without even a hint of light from within, so dark it could be the depths of outer space itself. For a moment, he reaches for the door frame and hangs on desperately. But something (hello again) begins to pry his fingers loose one by one. They twang as they release, spring open and then snap back once more—uselessly, grasping nothing. Finally, exhausted, panting with fright, he lets himself go and quickly falls in, miraculously landing on his feet as the room re-cants. Despite a dark so thick he can see but a few centimetres in front of him, he immediately knows this is no classroom. At least, not an ordinary one. No, he can smell the bedsheets, the baby powder, the over-starched laundry, the recently-percolated coffee, the aromatic pipe tobacco. He doesn't know when the voice started but it's definitely there now, behind him on the bed, telling him to relax, to let go. That voice, though roly-poly and jolly-good friendly, freezes him. His breathing is shallow and tight with fear; his heart is threatening to burst out; he is oozing sweat. A hand reaches around to undo his zipper, to slip into his trousers. The fingers are cold and uncaring. All the while the pipe glows and the voice drones on about how lonely the monastic life can be, how necessary it is to have company once in a while, how the Lord in His infinite wisdom and understanding forgives. Giulio can't fight back for some reason, although he knows he could easily fend the attacker off and make good his escape. Even inflict some damage, if he so wanted. But he doesn't. He simply acquiesces, simply allows things to happen—as if he has no choice in the matter.

Giulio always wakes up before ejaculation—I make sure of that.

But there are times when he can't help himself, when the process started in the dream spills over and he's left to wipe up the sticky mess. There follows a combination of disgust and elation, of warmth and fear, a devastating uncertainty as to the significance of these dreams. Is he victim or perpetrator? Why does he find himself enjoying and loathing it at the same time? Is he living a lie, a lifelong lie so deeply interred only the dung beetle larvae have been able to burrow their way down to it? These are exactly the reactions I'm looking for, that I want to elicit. Surprise, surprise.

Sometimes, as a way of appeasing his conscience, he tries to analyze the dreams based on the news of the day: stories of sexual molestation, abuse of trust and criminal charges in far-flung orphanages; immigrant fears of minority status and marginalization in a place Giulio has always considered home; editorials on steam-rolling bureaucracies, making it harder and harder to get to the core of things.

He may have a point. But I think that says more about me than it does about him. Besides, what would he do if he had a dream about .. oh, let's say purely for the sake of argument . . . stabbing his mother? About placing one knee on her chestbone and making a neat incision across her grizzled, wrinkly throat? About holding out the tin cup into which the rapidly-congealing blood drips with tick-tock timing? About watching her eyes make the slow, majestic turn inward as the body spasms and jerks? What would his excuse be then? Would he struggle to construct the correct analytic scaffolding? Would he reach back for some primeval Freudian analogy—Oedipus Regina for postmodern times? Would he, out of the blue, ask: which came first—the chicken or the mother? The mother or the egg? Or would he simply lean over and vomit on the spot—a gush that would slowly empty him from the inside out until even his loveliest organs hung there for all the world to see?

Hmmm. I wonder.

X. Upon his wife

Giulio loves his wife. At least, he says so at the drop of a hat—and that's good enough for me. The fact they haven't lived together for more years than either can recollect shouldn't be used to cast doubt—or aspersions—on such a statement. If love is more the memory than the presence, more the thought than the reality, more the wish than its fulfillment, then Giulio is overflowing with the stuff. "I love my wife," he'll say the moment a conversation even hints at approaching the vicinity of the subject of love and wives. There are photographs of her—both framed and unframed—all over the house (including the one with a plucked and gutted chicken perched on her head, Pope's nose above pert nose). He still has some of her clothing: in particular, panty-hose, a bra and other sundry pieces of female finery. These he stole before they split up for good, managing to squirrel them away while she had her mind on other matters. As well, the creaking bed in which he sleeps (and dreams) and the dilapidated dresser beside it—not to mention the major appliances in the rest of the house—are all things they had bought in those first heady days of their marriage. In the days when it was still the two of them doing battle against the world, when sex was a constant discovery and emotional investments came easily, as easily done as said. I guess the only thing missing really is his ever-beloved wife—and, to this day, he's not sure why that has happened. Or even when precisely.

Let's see now. Were they still together for the African sojourn? Yes. Yes, they must have been—at least for part of the time. Giulio can clearly remember (will never be permitted to forget) the cold fever of those nights under the mosquito netting. Cold? Those nights were swampish, stifling, suffocating; the air itself an impediment to breathing, a stiff, over-bearing board that pressed relentlessly against his chest. Pressed with all the weight of a world gone malarial. But it was cold, Giulio will swear to it. What else? The two bodies lying side by side but not quite touching, in close proximity but never in real contact. A golden cockroach slithering out of the faucet that only provided water at random during the day. The men, wisps of aromatic smoke escaping their burnooses, huddled together in the hotel courtyard, engaged in secret confabulation. The snapshot of a naked woman's back as she squats in the bath tub, splashing precious liquid between her thighs. The cat disgorging pieces of lizards as if they were its own guts. The watermelon bursting open, splitting apart to reveal a teeming army of caterpillars, ready to march and defoliate. The camels drooping out of the caravanserai, still weary, wavering, disappearing in the distance, swallowed by a dusty mirage that could very well have been the end of the world. A very fat, very angry viper hissing in a jam jar. All separated, cold, frozen in ice like fossils and sealed away in no particular order. These are the images that Giulio knows all too well. I've driven them into the deepest parts of his brain, have made them his own so completely he now believes he wouldn't be Giulio without them, now believes that, without them, he would fade away, de-materialize a piece at a time. And maybe he would.

But, at what point does Giulio's wife herself start to fade away, to de-materialize? Is it during one of their frequent dugout trips across a mud-swollen river, there one moment standing on the prow and gone the next—like the white-washed bridge that spans halfway and then stops dead, the exposed beams of concrete and steel slowly rusting in the damp-shrouded tropical air? Or it maybe along the Gboko-Jos road, lined with the hulks of decapitated Mammy Wagons and women holding their children up to be blessed by the passing car lights. Or on the white-powdered beach in Togo, a sun-bleached, rectilinear city shimmering behind them like the very ghost of colonialism. Perhaps, fully clothed, she suddenly dives into the water and swims for the luxury liner that is waiting several kilometres out, its Christmas lights blinking like a friendly giant's wink, its passengers prowling the deck in evening gowns and tuxedos. Yes, that may have been it. She has always been an extremely powerful swimmer, tireless, persistent, the kind of swimmer most often described as dolphin-like.

But the truth is Giulio doesn't know. When he tries to think about it, he draws a blank. Or maybe a blanket is more like it, a way to muffle himself from a pain he wouldn't be able to handle head on. For any everyday purposes, then, his wife is still there—even if only as a neural residue, the last drip-drip of a lost chemical-electrical activity. She represents the ultimate stage—of five—in the evolution of Giulio's sexual growth, the punctuated equilibrium that has narrowed his choices down to nil and which will soon have him a candidate for his very own fossil record. Ice cold and separately packaged, making it easier for others (like me) to chip away, to uncover what we've stored there in the first place. Ha, ha. Look what we've found. Surprise, surprise, surprise.

Here they are then, the . . .

FIVE ESSENTIAL AND ABSOLUTELY NECESSARY STAGES OF GIULIO'S SEXUAL DEVELOPMENT

1. **Puberty**: With the shouts of his classmates far below him, Giulio slowly climbs the gym rope, painfully hauling himself up hand over hand. At each upward shift of his body, he must place one foot sideways against the thick hemp to prevent a quick slide and the subsequent raw burns on his palms. For a moment, though, as he dangles some five metres above the floor, he releases his foot and hangs suspended, slowly twirling in the dust-encrusted fluorescent lights. It is then, barely a few moments later, that he feels a jolt along his sphincter, as if someone has eased a wet finger inside and is now massaging it back and forth. That is quickly followed by a sharp, exquisite pulsing at the base of his penis and a liquid-y befoulment into his gym shorts. Later, during those bedraggled, confused months of puberty, Giulio will often try to re-construct the conditions under which he first ejaculated—by hanging down from the roof of the garage, for example, with his pants around his ankles, or by hoisting himself up repeatedly on the playground monkey bars, toes barely off the ground. But, while these techniques work, at least enough to produce a simulacrum of the desired effect, nothing can ever replace that first rope: the feeling of rough fibre on his palms and the back-and-forth action of a smooth finger up his anus.

2. **Adolescence:** Out of the devilish, recessive dark they come, four abreast, the unremitting and eternal menaces, determined to beat the romance out of Giulio. But he stands his ground, takes his punishment like the proto-man he is becoming, feeling each hob-nailed boot penetrate his soft flesh, spare no rib, crack the hard shell of his skull. Clutching himself and crawling off, Giulio tries to make his way into the safety of the nearby fields, a place where the reeds still grow tall and straight, where the drops of blood cause the very ground to stir in sympathetic anger. There, he struggles to remain conscious, to await a re-working of the world into something grander, something more able and willing to support his not-so-graphic design. But it's a losing battle and, when he awakes, he finds himself lying in a hospital bed, head wrapped in bandages—and his soul-mate beside him, the woman who will tend to his wounds, whose flowery breath alone is enough to heal him. It's usually at this moment, as the shimmering, all-but-faceless lady leans over and sighs ever so sweetly, that Giulio, suddenly back in his own room, climaxes, making sure the semen spills onto a Kleenex or his own underwear, while he rubs himself against the mattress, eyes grimly shut, holding onto the moment for as long as he possibly can. He finds this a lot easier and less dangerous than hanging from gym ropes or the roofs of garages, pants around his ankles.

3. **Pre-Adult:** With the passage of time, however, the vision begins to wear thin. Giulio discovers one day that he can no longer hold it, that he tends to open his eyes in the middle of what should be a "beautiful moment", and that, horror of horrors, the exercise more often than not turns out in vain—a wilting. And that spells the end just as clearly as if the four menaces had really done him in. For, despite the purity of thought and ideals of chivalry he may have espoused, the ultimate object has always been to relieve himself in the most pleasurable way possible. If relief doesn't come, if there is no discharge of fluid. . . . This proves a difficult period for Giulio, of toothbrush experimentation and reversion to hairy ropes, of fecal exploration and oral frustration—all of which work to some extent but don't serve to bring back the old glory. And he flounders about for several months—until he

discovers the power of religious icon lust. Specifically, a portrait of the Virgin Mary behind glass which has hung above his bed for as long as he can remember. Approximately four inches wide by eight high, this can be held easily in one's hand and rubbed against the tip of the penis. The sensation is one of immense coolness, combined with the appropriate amount of sacrilege. And the thought of the Mother of God with her sanctified lips on <u>his</u> penis is more than enough to get Giulio spurting. After he makes his religious icon lust discovery, it irks Giulio to no end that he's wasted so much time on shimmering faceless ladies whose amorphousness allowed him wide play and the full spectrum of possibility but no direct contact. Of course, there is no direct contact in this case either, with the glass coming between his privates and the Virgin's immaculate, all-forgiving face. But, somehow, that only serves to increase the ultimate pleasure—and at the same time also serves to keep his disgust following the act down to a manageable level.

4. **Adult:** Giulio loses his passion for religion—and, by reduction, for religious icons—only after he meets his future wife. Now, with an actual woman beside him in bed (even if only for a short while), he has plenty of occasions to practice two-way, fully reciprocal sex. More importantly, it gives him the opportunity to become hands-on familiar with female anatomy and to add much-needed depth to his unfocussed imaginings. It is thus he enters the "glistening, well-oiled labia between high-ended buttocks" phase: maturity, in other words. During this period, his favourite position in bed (when not being shared by his wife) is with a full-colour centrefold poised on his legs: one hand on his penis; the other holding the well-worn, thumb-marked paper; and both eyes riveted to the spot framed so thoughtfully by the photographer. He finds this very comfortable, very natural. There's none of the physical strain associated with ropes. Or the mental gymnastics of creating ideal women. Or the emotional turmoil of trying to de-flower the Mother of God herself. The glossies were made for exactly this purpose, for the mature man to use when his wife—or woman of choice—isn't available. A variation on this is to lean over the toilet bowl with the top of

the tank providing a natural stand for the oversized spread. Aside from the strengthening of the leg muscles and firming of the stomach, an advantage of this position is that Giulio has nothing to clean up afterwards. A simple flush does the job swimmingly. And he can easily go for a quickie whenever he pleases as no one questions his use of the bathroom. In fact, come to think of it, it is probably during one of those quickies that his wife does the unconscionable and walks out on him. Perhaps, she even knocks on the door to bid him a teary good-bye and he tells her he'll be out in a jiffy—only to find her gone once he finally emerges, all refreshed and zippered up and with the glistening labia folded neatly in his back pocket.

5. **Post-Adult, Pre-Senility:** But no. Although he has now blanked the memory out completely, Giulio is fully aware of what is taking place at the moment his wife leaves him. In fact, he is sitting on his mother-in-law's coat-of-all-colours sofa at the time, reading . . . oh, let's say . . . a J.D. Salinger book. Not *the* J.D. Salinger book but one of the short story collections with the inspirational titles about carpenters and suburban suicides. And suddenly his wife starts to shout at him, as if it were the continuation of one or another long-standing argument. This puzzles Giulio as he isn't aware of any previous argument, long-standing or otherwise. Nevertheless, he puts the book down, making sure not to lose his spot, and follows his wife into the bedroom. She has already stuffed most of the clothes from the beat-up dresser into her suitcase and is busy working her way through the closets, all the while continuing her steady harangue on his faults, errors in judgement and general unwillingness to listen from the day when she'd first warned him their marriage was in trouble—or "in deep shit", as she puts it in her inimitable way. Of course, Giulio can't recall any such warnings—which only goes to further prove her point. In any case, she is about to embark on her last search pattern through the room when the radio suddenly comes on—Styx's overly-familiar but still seminal *Come Sail Away*—and, for some reason which even I have trouble explaining (sure, sure, you say—but I'm serious), Giulio decides to kick her last change of clothes under the bed. Then, he says, purely as

a further means of distracting her: "Isn't that just an awesomely inspirational piece of music? They don't make ballads like that any more, do they?" Instead of answering, his wife swears, angrily slams the "Off" button into a permanently depressed position, picks up their daughter and storms out, never to be seen again. Or at least with that intention. Giulio sits on the bed for a few moments, thinking thoughts such as: "Civility is the noblest of virtues except when practised between couples." Then, brushing aside some dust balls, he reaches tentatively underneath the bed. The clouds are immediately lifted. For, as luck would have it, he has managed to salvage a complete set of his wife's unwashed undergarments: silk panties, panty-hose and half-bra.

And Giulio is the first to admit that those undergarments sure have come in handy down through the years. For one thing, they've allowed him to forget that she's left him—for now she is always there whenever he needs her, whenever he's in danger of remembering that dark, misfired day when the boat went sailing out with only her on it. Granted, the scent gets weaker all the time, as if each sniff removes one more layer of precious pheromones. But Giulio doesn't really notice as he lies there with the panties orientated in a strategic manner across his face. And, as a last gesture of kindness on my part (to think some accuse me of cruelty), I'm going to make sure she lasts exactly as long as he does. That's right. With the two of them growing more and more faint together. Yes. More and more ethereal. More and more meaningless. Until those final few moments when, like the rest of you, he confuses ropes, romance, Virgins, labia and wives in a boffo performance just before the lights go out.

Or I switch them off. Or they run out of juice. Or the fuses blow. Or whatever.

XI. Farewell . . . or the extrapolation blues

While enjoying a quiet moment in the den of the drug kings, Giulio reflects on a recent incident that took place involving himself and his daughter. A little background: In one of my more mischievous moments, I envisioned what the poor child (barely past her teens) would look like as a full-fledged Jehovah's Witness. And then I liked her so much in the guise I decided to keep her that way for as long as humanly possible—with a few little quirks thrown in for good measure, of course. So now, blissfully oblivious of the fact it's *The Watch Tower* that needs peddling, she goes daily from house to house, *The Plain Truth* magazine in hand, submitting herself to every abuse possible for her adopted cause. Occasionally, she pays her father a visit, accepts his standing offer of coffee and biscuits and then plunges directly into the faith-versus-belief-versus-knowledge discussion that dominates all their conversations. She has long since given up trying to convert him or even to make him see her point of view. But at least here—in the house she left when she was barely of nursery school age—she knows what to expect. That allows her to dispense with the witless grin that creeps onto her face as she stands on the doorsteps of complete strangers, summer or winter, rain or shine, flood or snowdrift.

As a rule, Giulio also enjoys the company of his daughter whom, he feels, has turned into a kind and beautiful lady, caring of others and with an inner resolve that puts his lack of direction and motivation to shame. She reminds him of how things might have been, of the life he could have led: the family gathered around the solid oak dinner table; the wit and sparkle of their sophisticated talk; the tinkle of crystal glasses and genuine laughter; the full, clear, scratch-free tones of *The Ode to Joy* issuing from the compact disc player. This makes him nostalgic and all a-glow and tingly inside, even if it's only a reflected warmth from a fire that I've been busy fanning. The fake shadow of the fake lantern swinging against the projected wall of a cardboard cut-out of Plato's re-built-for-tourists cave and bed and breakfast emporium.

But, on this occasion, just as his daughter is about to launch into her latest defence of *The Plain Truth*, based on its repeated imperviousness to buckets of ice-cold water, rabid canines and threats of death at seven in the morning, Giulio confesses to her he is planning to kill himself. It's a spur of the moment decision on his part and (seriously) he's only half-serious. In fact, he hasn't even come up with a proper method yet and just wants to gauge her reaction. But the results are devastating; the reaction beyond anything he could have imagined in his worst nightmares—and that's saying something, as I can make his nightmares pretty devastating. Immediately, before his very eyes, his daughter begins to fade away to nothing as she looks at him wide-eyed from across the yellow kitchen table. Although Giulio gets the impression she's not actually vanishing, just slipping into another dimension perhaps, it makes little difference in practical terms. Another dimension is as good as nowhere if Giulio can't follow her. Naturally, he immediately regrets his spontaneous declaration to do himself in and tries to tell her it was just a bad joke on his part, ill-conceived and to be retracted at once. But it's too late to do anything of the sort. Unattended, the coffee cup rattles; the spoon slips to one side; the soggy biscuit topples over. In a final desperate effort to keep his daughter with him, he shouts, reaches out with both arms and attempts to hug her fiercely. And ends up hugging himself.

Being a rational, naturally curious man (as well as a terminally sympathetic character), Giulio tries to repeat the experiment—this time on the next-door neighbour with whom he's been conducting an on-again off-again affair for the past half-dozen years. They were introduced originally when she requested that he return a shirt blown off her line onto the tomato plants in his back yard. The handing back of that shirt—her husband's, by the way—started them down a secret path of afternoon trysts that has been made more creative and somehow less sordid by the fact she insists on evening wear no matter what the time or occasion. Originally, they worked out a plan whereby she'd come over whenever Giulio gave the all-clear signal (by leaning out his "illegal view" window and waving a Boy Scout kerchief in her direction). The woman soon began to question the purpose of the signal when she realized that Giulio, unlike her, lived alone. (What she couldn't possibly know, of course, is that Giulio doesn't realize he lives alone, that for him the affair is conducted as a polite menage à trois, with his wife as the silent, invisible but extremely co-operative third partner.) And so, lately, much to Giulio's chagrin, she has taken to ignoring his signals and dropping in whenever she feels like it, trench-coat concealing deep-slitted dresses or peekaboo lingerie ordered directly from the more risqué Hollywood houses.

It's on one of these afternoons that Giulio conducts his experiment. They are relaxing in bed together after the first torrid round, watching the tear-filled ending of the daily soap, when he substitutes his suicide intentions for the sweet nothings he normally whispers in her ear. At first, she giggles and rolls her eyes, telling him he's a great kidder—unlike her dour and sourpuss husband who laughs only at roadkill remnants and World War II carnage. Then, when Giulio insists he's serious, that he really means it, she gets into the act. She kneels down before him and mock pleads with him not to do it, while at the same time reaching into her trenchcoat for a second condom (a capot from her capot, as she calls it). But throughout it all, she remains as solid as ever—or as solid as middle-aged mid-sections and laissez-faire breasts will allow. No fading away for her; no evening gown left behind to take its place beside his wife's cherished undergarments. So much for that, Giulio thinks, as he eases himself into her from behind, fondles and French kisses his wife and then peers across his mistress's broad back at the last few moments of *Another World*. Falling away while the credits roll, he is left doubly disappointed. He had hoped to use this occasion both to prove a scientific point and to rid himself of what is quickly becoming a nuisance. Now, he'll have to resort to more prosaic measures—changing the lock, for instance. Or even moving altogether. But he doesn't think he can risk that, for fear his wife will also be left behind.

Matters aren't helped much when his daughter suddenly re-appears a week or so later, demanding her coffee and biscuits as if nothing untoward has happened. She is surprised at his show of emotion, at his insistence that they hug. He has always been reticent, not so much out of lack of feeling but from an excess, overly concerned about the other person's reaction to an overt emotional display. It's a deliberately un-Italian trait, born out of a morbid dread of stereo-typing (both his and mine).

His daughter submits to the hug. Then she tells him that the old woman who lived by herself across the street has died at last, hit by a car as she crossed against the light. Isn't life funny that way? Having reached the ripe old age of 82, everyone had naturally been concerned for her future welfare—in particular, where they would place her once she became incapable of taking care of herself. At least once a week, the ambulance would speed to her house, bringing much-needed oxygen and the company of others. And, although she still insisted on doing her own shopping and household chores, the family knew it was only a matter of time before the double canes would no longer be of any use. But no one suspected a teenager in a red convertible, unable to brake in time as the geriatric jaywalker stepped out from behind a parked bus. So her death came as a complete surprise after all. How does the daughter know all this, you ask. Why is she so au courant? It turns out the old lady was one of her first converts and, until her dying day, accepted *The Plain Truth* as the bible for modern living.

Giulio, on the other hand, claims not to know what his daughter is talking about. He says he's never seen any old lady on the street, let alone one who walks with double canes. His daughter drags him to the front window and points to a house directly across from him. See, they're moving out her furniture right now. All antiques and stained-glass, collectibles and silver tea sets from the time of Queen Victoria. See. Sure enough, a large van has parked diagonally on the road, its back end up against the house. Several men are bustling out brightly-polished appliances and gilded mirrors along a make-shift bridge from the front door to the van.

So, instead of solving the mystery, the return of his daughter has simply added one more. Several, as a matter of fact. The next time Giulio waves his Boy Scout kerchief out the back window, the only response he gets is from an unshaven, derelict-looking man who takes advantage of the illegal view to grin toothlessly at his neighbour. Giulio quickly ducks back in, thinking he has finally met his paramour's husband. But not so. The next day, a demolition crew arrives to tear down the obviously-abandoned home. They flush the derelict out and, chasing him with stones and curses, send him scurrying onto the street. And the street itself has changed as well. What had been mere days before a lower middle-class neighbourhood, complete with comfortable single-family homes and languid shade trees, is now an inner-city ghetto. Stripped-down cars squat engineless in puddles of thick oil; waves of refugees and the homeless fight each other for every square inch of free space; gangs of feral children roam the alley ways, trying to break into any unprotected home; broken pieces of glass sprout like demonic fingers along the tops of six-foot high concrete block fences; the manhole covers explode and steam rises from the sewers, bringing with it the sleek, pungent, finger-snapping odour of poverty mixed with a dash of official ignorance.

Giulio, having steel-plated both front and back doors and replaced glass panes with metal bars, sits huddled in his livingroom, trying to ride it out. But it doesn't prove possible. One day, as he waits by the window for the Brink's truck to deliver his weekly groceries, he spots four men engaged in unnatural activity right in front of his house. They're busy ripping the clothes from an unfortunate woman who has strayed into their path. He has witnessed such scenes before—raping and pillage being an essential part of any descent into chaos. But this time he can't sit calmly back and pretend nothing's going on. For, although he can only see the woman's back, he does recognize the distinctive clothing of a Jehovah's Witness and the book with which she is trying to fend off her attackers. Giulio screams out his daughter's name, rushes from his house and, without having really worked out the consequences, throws himself against the two men closest to him. Thus, in the confusion, he manages to save the intended victim and she escapes, holding ripped pieces of clothing against herself in a last-ditch effort at modesty. But Giulio isn't so lucky. He makes a dash for his house, only to realize that he has locked himself out—part of his burglar-proof system. Backed up against the front door by the group angry at being deprived of their prey, he shuts his eyes and reflects on faceless women in gossamer dresses. One at a time, the men take turns administering vicious kicks to the most tender parts of his body. Then, while the others prop Giulio up, the leader of the gang, whom he recognizes too late as the derelict-husband from next door, plunges a knife repeatedly into his stomach and leaves him for dead. The irony is that the woman turns out not to have been his daughter after all. And, if Giulio hadn't allowed himself to be so taken in by first appearances, he would have noticed that fact before he unbolted his door and ran out so precipitously. All he had to do was take a close look at her book as she swung it around. It was *The Watch Tower*. (My attempt at warning him, obviously. But much too subtle a clue, I guess, where raw human emotion is involved.)

In any case, everything seems to have been returned to its proper place: Giulio makes a miraculous recovery, although he now has a brand-new set of dreams with which to contend; the neighbourhood is back to its old self, with the refugees, the thugs and the homeless swept out of sight or swallowed by a resurgence of civic pride; both his daughters—the real one and the one he saved from a cruel fate—come by for visits and most often end up arguing with each other over who has the stronger faith; Giulio's affair with the next-door neighbour heats up again—she's particularly taken with the scars on his abdomen, which glow crimson when she passes the tip of her tongue over them, superimposing herself on his wife; and, last but not least, he's once more contemplating suicide—only this time he keeps it to himself, not willing to risk another sudden disappearance with all its attendant marvels.

Of course, if he had asked me, I would have told him straight out that his daughter's vanishing had absolutely nothing to do with what came later, that there was no cause and effect connection between the two. On the other hand, being a committed believer that things only happen for a legitimate reason, he probably would have scoffed at my attempts to explain: either, a) because that's the way I wanted it—and to hell with anyone who couldn't appreciate my sense of humour; or b) because I had some deeper, more mysterious plan concealed behind the apparently coincidental occurrences.

Besides, who's to say he wouldn't be in exactly the same position (at exactly the same table) in the middle of the night in the den of the drug kings? And who's to say his path there would have been any different? All I know is that he has exhausted virtually every means of doing himself in: from using a gym rope to hang himself to jumping out in front of a speeding pizza delivery car; from throwing himself out a seventh-storey window to swallowing several tablespoons of strychnine; from plunging into the frigid river off the edge of his island home to burying himself alive in an abandoned gold mine in the Northwest Territories. And the fact he's quietly contemplating life at this very moment is no guarantee that he failed at each and every single attempt—or that he failed at any of them. In fact, they may have all been successful for all he knows; they may have all ended with the cessation of his bodily functions, the shutting down of neural pathways, the explosion of blood vessels and snapping of neck vertebrae, the bulging of eyeballs in a last desperate attempt at a last desperate gasp of air; they may have all been followed by sobbing and a gnashing of teeth, by the final shower of earth slowly turning to mud as the very cosmos itself wept in sympathy.

But what may or may not have been really doesn't matter to Giulio. He's here now in the cave-like atmosphere, listening to the dealers and the addicts exchange notes, watching the comings and goings between bathroom and table. He himself is clutching the very same table with both hands, fearful that he'll float away if he lets go—and fearful that he won't, that he'll become so heavy as to sink right through the Earth's crust. One of his friends—dealer or addict or both, he's not sure and it doesn't really matter—walks over to the table and begins talking to him. Giulio nods, without understanding. Normally, he wouldn't even have to pay attention to grasp what the person across from him is saying. Having known most of the others since at least high school, Giulio has long before exhausted the repertoire of their conversation, long before circled every conceivable topic and worn it out to a comfortable triteness, to a series of grunts and nods and half-finished thoughts. In fact, on most nights, Giulio could walk in and respond to a question he hasn't even heard—or take over an argument at the exact point the previous speaker has left off (for another trip to the bathroom, no doubt). But it's not the same on this night—and it doesn't get any better as more and more join him at the table, patting him confidentially on the shoulder or giving him a friendly jab to the chest. Somehow, without realizing when it happened, Giulio has fallen out of the conversation and can no longer get back in. He looks around from one person to the other, faces bright and artificially alert, their mouths opening and closing in the dim light. Have they decided—all at once and in unison—to switch languages? To talk in private code? Could it be they've learned from reliable sources the table has been bugged by narks? Or is it simply a schoolyard game they're playing, exchanging vowels for consonants and adding unneeded endings? Whatever the case, it effectively excludes Giulio. He listens for a few moments more, at first worried about what is happening but then actually revelling in his sudden non-understanding. With an outrush of air, he lets go the table and pushes the chair back. Neither rising up nor sinking dramatically, he begins to walk away, his feet barely touching the drug den's sticky floor. Several of the patrons at the bar stop in mid-sentence and wave at him as he goes past. Then, they quickly turn back to arguing who was really the greatest left winger of all time (Guy Lafleur? Bob Gainey? Leon Trotsky?). On his way out, at precisely the moment he pulls open the bulletproof plate-glass front door, a man in a conical cap walks in. The man is carrying a plastic tray with one hand, holding it out in front of him like a ceremonial offering. On the tray lies a plucked, gutted, cleaned and decapitated chicken. Despite the fact the animal has been skewered through the anus to the base of the neck, and its leg stumps decked out with fancy gold ribbons, there are still signs of fresh blood on the tray, a drip-drip not quite congealed. The man stops to ask Giulio if he knows who placed the order. Giulio jerks his finger behind him without bothering to look back. The man doffs his cap and bows from the waist, then continues towards the table Giulio has just left. Giulio himself emerges from the den of the drug kings, goes up the few steps to ground level and, taking a deep breath, walks slowly down the pre-dawn boulevard, the beautiful leafy-green boulevard lined with sleepy birds on telephone wires and sentient rose bushes smiling just for him.

All the while he is thinking: Is this it then? Is this the night I've been so anxiously waiting for, the night I finally have my date with non-existence?

XII. Scenes from a life ... scenes from some deaths

At first, I was sorely tempted to leave Giulio at precisely that point, to let the word "non-existence" serve as a natural counterpoint to whatever essence may have been built up, accidentally or otherwise, in the previous pages. But the more I thought about it the more I was struck by the false sense of completeness and closure such an ending would give, as if something had finally been resolved, as if a series of suitably abstract premises had been brought to a suitably satisfactory conclusion. Not so suitable. So, instead, I've chosen to provide the reader with some seemingly random selections from Giulio's life, what used to be called vignettes, I guess, but which I prefer to label marginalia (as in *Margins And Borders*). By that I mean that they don't really fit anywhere in particular but can perhaps be understood as spin-offs or out-takes or stories without centres—if such a thing is indeed possible, if we don't fight tooth and claw to force a centre no matter what we've been told, to punch our own jagged holes wherever we may feel a need for them. I've selected eight in all and given them alphabetical identifications purely for the sake of keeping things as simple as possible. That one comes before the other is no indication of importance or relative value. Simply a fact of linear life. In fact, if it were possible to read them all at once, that would be the preferred method. Nor should any significance be attached to their number, lengths or sequence. And, if anyone should, despite everything, succeed in finding a pattern, they'd best keep it to themselves, best treat it as something that's of a purely private nature. It's precisely universality that I'm trying to do away with here.

· · · · ·

a. When it comes to the performance of acts of bestiality, imagined or otherwise, Giulio discovers that cats are much more easily handled than dogs. But that's not the same as easy to handle and it is best to make certain the cat in question has been either de-clawed or recently chloroformed—or you may be faced with a situation leading to unpleasant short- and long-term consequences. Aside from their use as objects for pleasure, cats can also come in handy as objects for torture, at least among children of a certain social background. Not counting the standard spinning and swinging games, the tossing and kicking sports, Giulio still remembers vividly three particularly vicious forms of torment inflicted on cats during his youth. One consisted of holding a cat down and inserting a HB pencil into its rectum (making it, I suppose, an object that combines both sexual and torture elements). Another brought together the sharply-reacting alliance between a cat's tail and a lit string of firecrackers— the old style firecrackers that exploded with vicious effectiveness and sometimes took eyes and fingers along with them. The third was the most diabolical of all. It required the suspending of two cats from the top and bottom parts of a clothes-line—or from two side-by-side clothes-lines—and then slowly bringing the hissing screeching spitting creatures into close proximity. Repeatedly. Until the fur literally flew or the torturers lost interest. Now that Giulio thinks about it, there was a fourth: the chili pepper trick. A chili pepper was well hidden inside a cat's favourite tidbit, which was then innocently offered with an air of nonchalance. The fun consisted in watching the post-prandial cat trying to drown itself in the nearest barrel of rain-water. But this fourth form of feline torture was more an old man's demented pastime than a youngster's true delight.

· · · · ·

b. Giulio has been trying for years to become invisible—or rather to be seen strictly through his aura without the shoddy and distorting prism that is his body. And, when the commuter train comes out of the dark tunnel at last, a burst of multi-coloured light gives him the impression he has finally achieved that goal. But no such luck, however. It is only a cruel trick of the late afternoon sun as it reflects off the mica chips that are scattered about the railroad tracks. A quick blink of his eyes, a shake of the head and everything is back to a depressingly normal state. Why, after so many previous failures, after years of disappointment and embarrassment, he expects to suddenly become invisible in the middle of a holiday in the Roman countryside I really don't know. Perhaps he's hoping that way to avoid having to re-learn the language of his birthplace after being out of touch for so many years. Or he might want to become the ultimate tourist: a glowing presence felt but not seen, a fluorescent-markered query on someone's reservation list, a voyeur par excellence. In any case, they've now come to the end of the line and Giulio disembarks with the rest of the visitors at the small seaside town of Ostia, famous once as imperial Rome's port of choice. The streets, though paved, are covered with a soft, fine sand and he can hear the spray as it hits the beach. He removes his shoes and begins to walk towards the sound. Soon, the waves are mixed with children's laughter, the squeals of teenagers playing watery tricks on each other, the monotone of the spumone vendor. Giulio walks past what looks like a giant gazebo where loving couples lean with their elbows on glass-topped tables, staring at one another and languidly sipping espresso. Soon, he is standing well away from the developed area of the resort, on a grassy dune that slopes directly into the sea. The underside has been cut away through the action of the tide so that where Giulio is standing is actually a protruding lip, like that of a perennial pouter. There are signs warning about getting too close to the edge—and deep, wide tire tracks that must have been made by large trucks, the kind with hydraulic dumping mechanisms. Giulio kneels down and leans over the side. From there, he can clearly see, in the water below him, the remnants of white statuary, all in a jumble. The pieces are chunky and limbless, mostly stumps and torsos— and definitely unperipatetic. Yet the action of the water makes it seem as if they're moving. Back and forth and back and forth in the sinuous fashion of the idle rich. Giulio kneels there for most of the afternoon without gaining any further insight. Then, as the sun slants over the sea to the West, as the gazebo lights flicker on, as the children are pulled kicking and screaming from the water, as the moths rush for their momentary fix, he gets up and makes his way back to the patiently-waiting train, remembering at the last moment to brush away the sand between his toes before replacing his shoes.

· · · · ·

c. On one of those wintry afternoons when the sun is about to
set (before, it seems, it has even had a chance to rise properly),
Giulio comes to the conclusion that it might be interesting to
catalogue all his worldly goods. Besides, it's always a good idea
to know what you have on hand, he tells himself, what you can
rely on in a pinch. That way you can tag each item for future
reference and recall it without having to start the search from
the beginning. It also makes for less bickering when the relatives
come to divide the recently departed's possessions. But, because
he has so little, it doesn't take him long to complete the inventory: some clothing and clothing accessories; cutlery, glasses and
kitchen ware for two; a few pieces of crippled furniture; a TV,
stereo equipment, toaster, microwave oven; a manual typewrit-
er collecting dust; a print of Dali's *Inventions of The Monsters*; a
lamp with its shade looking like stretched skin; and an electric
fondue set, given to him by his best man as a wedding gift. The
only real decision he has to make is whether or not to include a
book he borrowed from the school library more than 30 years
before. He finally ends up putting an asterisk beside it. No sooner has Giulio finished his inventory than he notices how ster-
ile and underwhelming this catalogue truly is. It just sits there,
not even able to resonate with what Giulio feels he has invested
in these materials. So he tries something else—to work out the
relationships between and among the various objects he has ac-
cumulated. He quickly discovers that, while the objects may be
finite, the combination of relationships in no time tends towards
the infinite—especially if one includes reciprocity. Of course,
how many of these relationships are actually valid—can a toaster "love" a pair of silk panties? what does it mean when a fondue
set asks a lounge chair to slow dance?—is another question. But,
when trying to create a list of relationships, you can't stop to
work out which are plausible and which will never take place
no matter how many times the objects are thrown together. You
must include them all—or none. One thing is certain: simple
tagging is no longer possible. That would become a never-ending task. Instead, Giulio must resort to formulas and equations
of the general type: X_1 is P_1 to X_1, where 'X_1' is an instantiation

of any object over the range X and 'P₁' is a particular instance
of any relationship over the range P. Despite its clean feel and
logical crispness, its ease of handling and manipulation, this reduction to mathematical abstractions isn't quite what he had in
mind when he started the exercise. So Giulio sits and stares out
at the snowy afternoon, waiting for the sun to set. Then, at the
end of the day, he places his list of objects and relationships in
the microwave and blasts them to a fine powdery ash. Finally, he
shuts his eyes as tight as possible and concentrates on the explosions of light behind his eyeballs.

· · · · ·

d. . . . a ship or ship-like structure floating in a sea of quicksilver
. . . or mercuric chloride, to be more precise . . . the sky a slate-
grey wall . . . the horizon dripping red . . . Giulio, dressed in an
outfit that resembles an astronaut's spacesuit to protect himself
from the fumes, moves slowly from deck to deck. His face is flat
against the visor; his eyes unnaturally large, made strange by the
thick glass. In his claw-like hand, he holds clamped a faded photo of a young woman with two small children on her lap. Unlike
his, her eyes are straightforward and austere; her face round and
smooth; her hair tied back in a perfect bun. Though the photo
is black and white, someone has tried to apply a touch of red to
her cheeks. But it's obvious she's of peasant stock and has never
used rouge on her face—or deodorant for her under-arms. Giulio continues to move through the ship, now going from cabin
to cabin, throwing open each door in turn. Nothing. They are all
empty, the blankets on the cots folded neatly, the chamber pots
spotless. The doors begin to swing back and forth, creating a fu-
rious wind. Clanging, Giulio climbs back above deck. He cranes
his neck to look up. The clouds are now moving at impossible
speeds and bolts of yellow lightning pass between them—as if
in the midst of a celestial war. Accidentally, the clamp disengages
and Giulio drops the photo. As he tries awkwardly to retrieve it,
the wind picks it up and sends it skimming along the deck. He
thinks he has it once when it catches the edge of a rusted chair.
But before he can stoop down, the photo scurries away again.
Giulio gets one last chance as it wraps itself around the bow railing. He sneaks up behind it, afraid that one overly-heavy step

will dislodge it. He's there now, his hand reaching down for the photo's inviting edge. But the clamp doesn't have the finesse to perform such an operation and, instead of plucking the photo to safety, helps flip it through the railing. Giulio is left standing helpless as the faces bubble and fume in the corrosive bath.

· · · · ·

e. After watching the agonizingly slow death of a bull elephant on the *Best of National Geographic*, his all-time favourite TV show, Giulio has one question to ask: Can necrophilia ever be condoned? In this case, the young male elephants of the herd took turns mounting the dead leader while the melodic melancholic voice-over said they were both paying homage and letting the fallen know he was no longer the boss, that the party was definitely over for him. Giulio himself has never knowingly engaged in necrophilia—not even in his dreams. But he does have a friend who continued to make love to a woman even though she'd suffered a fatal stroke in his arms. Giulio has refrained from asking him how those final moments felt. Or even whether he'd noticed anything different. On another occasion, Giulio went to see what had been labelled as an art movie and multiple award winner on the international festival circuit. In one of the film's scenes, the two lovers reached the heights of ecstasy while one slowly strangled the other to death with a silken red scarf. Giulio thinks this is similar in some respects to his childhood rope-dangling trick. Only the stakes are higher because we're talking about consenting adults who are naturally more jaded. Of course, there's a vast difference between pure necrophilia and the killing of a partner while in the heat of love-making. For necrophilia to be that and nothing more, one has to come across the body—as if by accident. (Oh, look, simply perfect. I hadn't been counting on this but since it's there—what the heck. No point wasting a perfectly good body.) Or the killing itself must have nothing to do with the consequent act of sexually ravaging the body. That's why necrophiliacs are often disguised as soldiers. The danger, of course, is that conditions have a tendency to change really quickly on the battlefield and the potential necrophiliac can in no time become the sullen object of desire. So perhaps a better place would be the morgue—all those cooled down ex-humans, mostly the victims of horribly violent crimes or simple tiredness, being kept on ice. Although that, too, isn't without its dangers. At the top of the list is an overly-fastidious or jealous attendant locking in the necrophiliac; less likely but still to be considered is a seminal re-awakening of one of the ex-humans: OK, you've had your fun; now it's my turn. For those who don't actually like to handle the body while in the throes, there's always the secret viewing room at the local funeral parlour. For a price, most burial directors are more than willing to install a two-way mirror in the bathroom stall that directly overlooks the coffin. Giulio thinks about all this as he re-runs the tape of his favourite TV show. In fast-forward mode, the behaviour of the young bulls loses all majesty, becomes a farcical series of mountings and dismountings, intermingled with the proddings of sharp tusks and the incessant swirl of flies, vultures, hyenas and jackals all waiting their turns. But, no matter how often he watches the action—and at what speed—Giulio still doesn't know what any of it is supposed to signify or mean. So, could be he understands after all. Could be. On the other hand . . .

· · · · ·

f. It's as if everything has suddenly been displaced—by only a few millimetres perhaps but not so little as not to be obvious to the observant eye. And Giulio is nothing if not the possessor of a keenly observant eye. Actions repeat themselves in triples in the interval of the displacement—like a series of superimposed colour photographic plates not quite aligned. So he sees thrice in rapid succession his wife rush to the aid of the fallen motorcyclist. And thrice the limping victim leans on her shoulder as she leads him to the communal table. It's a gesture any decent human would be glad to repeat as many times as called upon, let alone the three on this occasion. But Giulio feels only a surge of bitterness that literally brings the bile to his throat. He swallows the acrid liquid—the remnants of mackerel patties and omelette. Later, he lies alone in bed, listening to the mosquitoes buzzing against the net. They too are lonely, he thinks—and out for blood. And, when his wife finally returns sometime in the middle of the night, it's still as if she's not there, as if her presence has become of no consequence. In the equatorial moonlight, he watches her crawl beneath the netting and sit for a moment on the edge of the bed. Then, with a sigh, she leans back in stages, cascading onto the pillow, parts of herself catching up with the rest a split-second later. Now, Giulio watches her out of the corner of his eye as she stares at the top of the net. His thoughts turn to tumbu flies and their larvae, the habit they have of hitching rides on clothes left out to dry and then burrowing deep into the skin, working their way sometimes right to the bone. He wonders what she's thinking about. Chances are good it's not tumbu flies but it could be anything: from finding herself sharing the meat market with vultures first thing in the morning to counting the number of days before she can go home. I could easily open up her mind to him, of course, expose the silliest whim, the most serious complaints, the deepest desires and wishes, the volcanic hatreds ready to explode. I could cup it in my hands like one would the end of a cold watermelon. Or a frisky kitten. But Giulio doesn't want to hear of it. He's deathly afraid of what he might find there—or not find there. He prefers instead to swallow his bile—and to lie awake nights watching her watching the top of the mosquito netting.

· · · · ·

g. Out of nowhere (well, not quite) the questions come popping—like soapy bubbles?—into Giulio's mind. Now, these aren't ordinary questions such as: How's the weather? And: Hey, how're you doing? No, these are questions Giulio has never even considered possible, let alone thought of asking: So, does essence, eh, come before existence? Can it—essence, I mean—"exist" without a body, a physical form? Conversely ("conversely", now there's a neat word), is there an essential part to a human being, without which he or she might still seem the same but wouldn't be a human being in some fundamental way? What would happen, for example, if you could perform a thought experiment where you would pare away a human's externals—limbs, flesh, muscle, bone, organs, brain, etc.—without hurting the essential person? For how long could that person continue to reflect on what is taking place: "Oh look, ma, now they've thoughtfully cut off my balls—but that's okay because, inside, heck I'm still me"? When would the essence be pierced, assuming there was such a

thing to pierce? Giulio, of course, is unaware that these are highly technical questions, debated in various forms throughout the
history of philosophy. And, although the words are similar to
those we use on a day-to-day basis, they develop a specialized
meaning during these debates, carrying the weight of centu-
ries—nay, millennia—on their shoulders. And, in the end, make
about as much sense as inquiring after the weather. Giulio, of
course, has asked them in pure innocence and has no idea what
he's getting into as he walks down the middle of the busy avenue, which has been closed off to traffic for the annual street
sale. Consequently, the merchants have pushed their stalls right
out onto the street, leaving but a narrow space in the middle
for pedestrians. Giulio stops to fondle a miniature statue of the
Buddha, which doesn't look at all out of place next to out-take
posters from Madonna's *Truth or Dare* movie. The statue is jet
black and the line of the mould can be clearly seen. Above its
head is a little ring through which a key chain can be inserted. Or
someone may wish to have it dangling from the front mirror of
the car as a good luck charm. After examining the statue carefully, Giulio replaces it and continues down the street. One of the
merchants is offering a pony ride and squealing children have
lined up to wait their turns. Another has go-carts with oversized
bumpers which speed along their predestined courses without
a single deviation—over and over in figure eights, which is the
symbol for eternity (just thought I'd throw that in there). A man
in a motorized wheelchair zooms by. He's carrying a boom box
which, regardless of the fact it can be heard for several blocks,
has been placed right up against his ear. Giulio then passes an
elderly but evidently still spry couple. They're practising their
tango steps, easing themselves back and forth from sidewalk to
street, from street to sidewalk like the semi-pros they've become.
The woman has her eyes shut and thus develops a dreamy quality about herself; the man wears light-brown checked pants and
two-tone shoes. You can tell they're used to being the centre of
attention and would be equally at home at a Club Med resort, a
tour of Greek temples or on a weekend sugaring-off trip to Par-
ent, Quebec. Wherever he looks, Giulio finds more fodder for
his imagination and descriptive powers. For example, a dozen

or so day-patients from the local psychiatric hospital are being led down the middle of the street. Although nothing physically divides them from the rest of the browsers, one can immediately pick them out: the shuffle, which eventually wears out the instep of their shoes; the look in their eyes like permanent reflectors; the not knowing what to do with their hands so that they either dangle clumsily by their sides or fly off in every direction. Giulio finds all of it fascinating. It also helps to keep him distracted. But, despite the plurality, the multiplicity of events taking place around him, Giulio isn't destined to stay ignorant for long on the subject of essence and existence. In fact, he's on the verge of finding out more than he'll ever want to know about this peculiar tandem. More than is really good for him, actually.

• • • • •

When Giulio decides on a lovely summer morning never again to leave his house, the first thing to suffer is the little patch of garden in the backyard. Not much to begin with, it is quickly over-run by weeds and insects, brightly colored creatures with voracious appetites for both food and space. As he lies in bed, getting up only to eat and to perform other semi-automatic functions, Giulio can observe from his window this return to chaos. This brings to mind another summer and another garden gone to ruin—that of his father. But, while Giulio's consists mostly of scraggly tomatoes and deformed, barely recognizable cucumbers, his father's garden was a thing of beauty and precision. Aside from the various types of tomatoes (rose and cherry, to name but two) and cucumbers (climbing, crawling, dangling), there followed row on row of neatly-trimmed pepper plants, onions, garlic, lettuce, cabbage, peas, several varieties of beans, broccoli, cauliflower, squash, zucchini, celery and egg-plant. Not to mention a grape trellis, apple, plum and pear trees and the pièce de resistance: a fig tree right at the centre, a fig tree which had to be completely buried each winter because it wasn't really meant to grow in such a harsh clime and should never have been submitted to these indignities in the first place. Giulio had seen his father dedicate himself entirely to that garden (like a religion), starting with the carefully-tended boxes of seedlings which he nursed in the greenhouse during the unpredictable days of early spring, through the planting process itself and into the nurturing needed to assure healthy growth.

So it came as an unpleasant surprise when, visiting for the first time in several weeks, he noticed a shagginess that hadn't been there before, a slight lengthening of the hair over the collar in a person who normally made weekly trips to the barber. It seemed that, for no obvious reason, his father had suddenly lost interest—this after more than seven decades of performing the same ritual cycle, the peasants' unschooled version of Persephone and the pomegranate seed, coaxing the cold, reluctant earth to yield its secrets one more time. When Giulio asked his father why, he simply shrugged, said re-birth was no longer important and went back to reading his illustrated history of the rise and fall of Mussolini. Not a month later, he was dead, stricken by "red wine disease," a lifetime's accumulation of poison in the pineal body—or, at least, that's what the doctors said. With his death, the reversal of the garden began in earnest. There was no stopping the waves of crab-grass, dandelions, milkweed and bramble bushes in their invasion of the well-fertilized and manured earth. They'd been waiting on the fringes for over six decades. As the fruits and vegetables strangled and rotted, the insects moved in, fearless now, not concerned about a sudden spray of green, metallic pesticide that gleamed copper sparkles in the sunlight. Ear-wigs, slugs, snails, beetles, tomato bugs, potato bugs, millipedes, tent caterpillars, aphids, ants, grubs of all kinds—they all began to eat, to suck, to chew so loudly they could be heard kilometres away—in Giulio's sleep even. And the milkweed pods exploded, the bramble bushes fired off their prickly seeds, the dandelions fluffed lady-like into the air. It was all over in a matter of weeks. The garden was no longer recognizable. Oh, if some one searched closely enough, they might still find a few cherry tomatoes hidden away, a crawling cucumber or two, a pepper burnished in hues of red and yellow. But chances were pretty good that, on turning the produce over, they would have noticed that the bottoms had been eaten away, the guts exposed, and the culprit still merrily and unconcernedly at work. Still later, as summer turned to fall, there came the rattle of the dry husks that had been left tied to their stakes with strips from old dresses and aprons. And then Giulio turned up one day after a bitterly cold night to witness the final demise of the fig tree. It had risen above it all till then, bravely putting out its succulent, erotic fruit as it waited patiently to be buried. But now it was drooped over, face to the ground, having succumbed to the first probing fingers of a frost that was destined to be permanent. And much more so than when he had stood viewing the body in the funeral parlour, Giulio knew then his father was gone.

Giulio's own garden doesn't arouse any of the passion or nostalgia of that long ago one. He simply watches with fascination its passing and dutifully notes the dates: "Today, the tomato plants can no longer be seen, having reverted to their wild state; the cucumbers, on the other hand, seem to be sprouting cancerous growths, knobby appendages, predatory pustules. It's the air pollution, combined with the alchemical action of industrious nature. It's the spirit of failed experimental medicines dumped into the nearest river—or the tributary closest to the nearest river. I fear at this point benign neglect isn't enough. I must get out and destroy them before it's too late. I must chop them into tiny bits and then transmogrify those bits in the microwave. Else they'll start to affect the other plants around them, perhaps causing a general revolution that can't be stopped, that'll over-run us all." But he does nothing of the kind, preferring to remain in bed. And, in this matter, I neither encourage nor discourage him. This is strictly his decision.

Because he will not venture out, someone brings him the food required for him to satisfy his daily caloric requirements. It could be his daughter. Or his next-door neighbour. Or even his ex-wife who comes to the aid of her stricken once-time husband with the same altruistic motives that had caused her to lend assistance to a wounded motorcyclist so many years ago. Whoever it is, the person rings the door-bell three times and then leaves without hesitation. Giulio will not answer if the food-bearer hangs around. On his way to opening the door, he passes a stack of mail which is getting larger and more unruly every day. In that stack, amid solicitation letters for Save The Earth and invitations to neo-Nazi rallies, can be found dire warnings from the various utilities. These utilities are patient, hoping he'll eventually come to his senses. They don't relish the thought of cutting off anyone's electricity, gas or telephone these days. It has more to do with maintaining their status as monopolies than any real concern for the clientele they serve. But that patience is running thin and the day fast approaches when Giulio will find himself shivering in the dark and the upturned phone emitting an unnatural silence, a suddenly failed carrier of external messages.

On the other hand, it might never get that far. An official-looking person might show up at his door at any moment now, read something out in a clear, clipped and appropriately loud voice, and then proceed to unscrew the hinges with an electric drill, battery-powered just in case. That person will have been sent by someone with only Giulio's interest in mind—his Jehovah's Witness daughter, his estranged wife, the broken-hearted next-door neighbour. They'll want to take Giulio away, to a place where he can be helped, where he can unburden himself in the company of others like him, those who don't know what to do with their hands, perhaps. Or who shuffle from one side of the room to the other in eternal puzzlement. This is only natural: we all seek to put away the ones we love.

Just as naturally, this is not what Giulio wants. He wants only to lie in bed, to eat occasionally if not regularly, to bathe when necessary and to use the toilet. Of course, those who come for him will tell him that's exactly what he'll be able to do at his new place of residence, at the group abode they've selected for him. But he's not sure he can believe them—and, based on past experience, I don't blame him. More likely, this obsession for staying in bed will be treated, first and foremost, as a way to escape reality, the lazy man's wish-fulfillment factory deluxe. Then comes the illness phase, the psychic probing to determine what could really be the matter, what could have gone so wrong as to result in this sad condition. So, while those who would like nothing better than to run an ultra-marathon are being kept sedated and practically strapped to their beds, Giulio can look forward to precisely the opposite treatment—and lucky if he even has a bed in his room. "Whatever you do, don't let him fall asleep," the out-going orderly will whisper to the in-coming one as they punch the time clock, speaking as if Giulio weren't even there. "Don't allow him to close his eyes. We might not be able to wake him up again."

It would seem that, despite Giulio's extreme reluctance to participate in this exercise, he won't have any choice when the front door comes crashing down, its descent softened by the burgeoning pile of mail. Having been stung in the past by a sudden attack of cleverness, those who come for him will also have someone waiting at the back door, their nets stretched to the utter limit after having climbed over the glass-topped fence and beaten a path through the rebel cukes.

So it would seem there's no way out for our sympathetic character, trapped by his own inability to be inconsistent, no matter how much the world around him makes sport and plays games that smack at first of the deepest import but which, in the end, mean sweet fuck all.

And, in case you haven't noticed, that really irks me. That's why I won't allow it. That's why, at the last moment, as the front door collapses, as the sweet voices waft in on waves of utter reasonableness, as the three ladies peer in all smiles and hopefulness, I invoke a previously unmentioned prerogative and create what has been until now an unknown escape hatch for my Giulio. It's through the basement, naturally, at the far end of the basement. Where the cobwebs are thick and steely enough to stop marauding bats. Where the bloodied writing remains curdled on the wall. Where a damp, pre-matrimonial mattress still has the indents from their original love-making. (Ah, what bliss, the dust that we made rise in the slanting rays of sun.) Now, the same people who had wanted Giulio captured are waving at him, urging him on, giving him hints and indications, signs and directions: a paraplegic in a wheelchair spinning his wheels; a dog shrugging off a thick layer of snow; an old woman expertly wielding a sharp feather; a red-faced man with a debased coin in his hand; another man who parts his hair to the left; a nuclear family shaking away the blues; a smiling God in a bloody smock smoking an aromatic pipe; a blonde child trying on a matched set of black angel wings; an hermaphrodite in a cylindrical cap; the parts and pieces mixing and matching, matching and mixing. And then melding precipitously into one, into one multi-dimensional creature.

They're all waving. Or is it one giant hand waving?

Giulio is polite enough to wave back, polite enough to acknowledge his departure—and then steps out through the crumbling wall.

Into what?

The preparatory cage, the ante-room for a never-ending torture chamber, so tight bits of his flesh protrude through the chicken wire?

Into what?

The infinite beach at the end of the albatross's runway, half-covered in sand and detritus but overpowering nevertheless in its filtered beauty?

Into what?

The busiest stretch of roadkill highway, melting into slippery and painful disrepair?

Into what?

The mournful, glad, sad, belated bedroom eyes of last week's serial killer?

The frozen flames of paradiso?

Of purgatorio?

Of inferno?

The sweet dragon's breath of birth?

All of the above?

Yes, of course.

And none?

Right again.

XIII. The extrapolation blues . . . or farewell. . . .

So, Giulio's managed to escape me. Managed to slip my grasp.

Well, not for long. He can't go very far—or long—without me. He's like a dog trained on a leash. After a while, it doesn't matter if it's around his neck or not. The only thing that counts is my voice. My tone of voice. The re-assurance in my tone of voice, letting him know there's someone here who cares for him and won't allow him to go astray. Or the note of anger, a sign of my displeasure. Or the occasional friendliness to soothe the choker's chafing.

Giulio, are you out there?

No response. But that's okay. I'll let him bounce around for a while. I'll let him discover for himself what freedom really means: life without my safety net to catch him when he falls; a world where the wounds—be they self-inflicted or the action of others—are often fatal. And then, all I have to do is whistle and he'll come running back to me. No matter where he might be. No matter how far away he finds himself. All I have to do is say the word and he'll be squatting by my side once more. Out of breath and panting slightly. But happy. Oh so happy. Like a good little puppy. Like the good little puppy dog he was trained to be.

It's as simple as that.

Really.

You'll see, Giulio. You'll see.

Giulio, are you out there?

If you are, let me know. You'll let me know, won't you?

Of course, you will.

Giulio, are you out there?

INTERMEZZO II: Moving off

Giulio. That's right. On the other side. From the other side. Across the other side. Whatever. How did I get here? You sent me here. Remember? I was "polite enough to wave back" and then stepped "out through the crumbling wall". Why? You're asking *me* why? That's rich. That's absolutely amazing. You don't know? You seriously don't know? I don't believe you. You're lying again—I just feel it. Besides, you never could tell the truth. It's one thing you never learned to do. Bah—it doesn't matter. I'll explain it to you anyway. I'll shine a light on a few of those cobwebbed corners. Whether you like it or not. For some reason, you thought I needed to escape. You thought *they*—whoever *they* might be—were coming to take me away. Ha, ha. Hee, hee. Ho Ho. To the funny farm. You thought they wanted to tie me down. To bring me back to my senses. To re-awaken the reality that was slowly abandoning me. To force me to get a grip on things. Or whatever name you want to give that everyday routine that eventually comes both to define and destroy us. But they weren't really coming for me, were they? Not for me at all. They were coming for you. It was you they wanted all along. And you knew that, too, didn't you? You knew from the very beginning exactly what you were doing. They wanted to toss that nice, little, fine-meshed net of reality over you and you—tricky, tricky you—managed to divert it. At the last moment, you managed to slip out. Using the oldest ploy in the world. It's him, you shouted, pointing at me with properly shaking finger. He's the one you want. He's the one in need of help. Look at the way he keeps his doors locked. Chained. Sealed. Nailed shut. Look at the way he lies in bed all day long. Unmoving. Staring at the ceiling. Stroking the base of his penis as if it belonged to someone else. Look at the way he doesn't eat, doesn't bathe, doesn't answer the phone, doesn't pick up his mail, doesn't respond to the voices and concerns of those around him, doesn't acknowledge love. I'm really worried about him. Sure, sure. And there I was all the while, stuck under your thumb. My lips zipped shut. Unable to make any rejoinder, unable to react, unable to explain myself. Why? Because you didn't want me to. Because you wouldn't allow it. Because what you said, what you wrote down, what you edited, what you crossed out and re-wrote, that was the law. My thoughts didn't count. My desires weren't even considered. My wants and needs were worth less than those of a mosquito flitting along a storm window screen, looking for some way in before the rain and the thunder and the lightning struck, washing it away forever with the other flimsy detritus. So, what do you say? Does that sound about right? Close to the mark? Close enough, eh. Come on. Admit it.

What! Oh, so now you're apologizing. Isn't that grand. Isn't that just peachy keen. Well, you can forget it. There's no way you're ever going fool me again with that ploy. No damn way. You've apologized before, haven't you? Many, many times before, if memory serves. When you wanted something from me, when it was to your advantage to appear meek and humble, when you had no other choice. And each time you reneged the moment it became possible, the moment I granted you pardon. Each time you got what you wanted out of me—worship, respect, forgiveness, some type of acknowledgement—and then tweezered me back into the jar. Like a prized specimen (oh, yes, I remember the butterflies). So why should I believe you this time? Why should I take your word for anything? Why should I even listen to you? You didn't know it at the time but, in your rush to get your pursuers off the trail, you actually did me a favour. A big favour. I'm on the other side now, the safe side. I can shut you off. Or up. Or out. Or in. Even in. If I don't listen, if I don't perform a snappy "Zieg Heil!" to your every command, it doesn't matter any more. There's no way you can get to me. Or at me. The tweezers turn to rubber the moment they cross this wall. They bend back on themselves. The orders, once so urgent and immediate, fall like shrivelled thistles by the wayside. The words themselves—"mother", "subway", "weddings"—have lost the power to coerce. Now, you're the one who's trapped, aren't you? You're the one unable to escape. And *they* didn't have to come for you after all. It wasn't necessary. Admit it. You managed to ensnare yourself, to cast the net over yourself. You spent so much time creating a miserable failure of a life for me you forgot to take care of your own. You forgot to notice your own was slipping inexorably away from you. You had a family once, didn't you? Oh yes, you did. Don't try to deny it. Let's see now: a loving wife; some proper number of children; a pleasant and spacious home; a respectable job; the opportunity for prolonged normalcy. And, while you were busy sticking it to me, the family left, tired of your lack of response, tired of the ghost that had replaced their husband, their father. And the job vanished. And then the pleasant, spacious home was gone, haunted. The opportunity for normalcy became the start of a horror show where everything sane came back twisted and tortured to remind you of what you'd done. How do I know? Well, you can't spend your time probing my psyche without leaving yourself open to some probes of your own. You can't expect to gain control over others without showing your own weak points. And now, you're all alone—and you don't even have me to kick around any more. Presto poof! The magic is gone and the jar is empty.

And don't waste your time trying to resurrect some of the other people you conjured up for me, some of the secondary characters you thought might enrich my all-too-pre-determined life: Paraplegic Pagan; my emotional rapist of a mother; my ever-leaving wife (or wives); my raging and ranting father; my soft afternoon mistress; my Jehovah's Witness daughter; my so-called dying friend: these and all the other pseudo-companions marching alongside me but to the beat of *your* drumming. Now that I'm gone, they're gone too, aren't they? Each one has slipped into their own "other side". When you turned the final page on me, you turned the final page on all of us. Oh sure, if you wanted, you could start up some new ones, begin again from scratch. But don't expect them to be the "new" old me—or the "new" old anyone else who has gone before. That's just not possible. And you know it, damn you. You could even give them the same names, the same features, the same feelings, the same reactions to "life's bitter ironies". But it still would be them and not us. We could not, no matter how hard you tried, inhabit the same word of the same sentence of the same page. Nor does it help for you to simply duplicate letter for letter what you've already written before, to say again, for example: "Giulio's mother, I write in my cramped style, in my cramped, ever-so-peculiar style, Giulio's mother showed him the reality in dreams." For that would quickly become meaning-less, that would quickly become an endless line of monkeys hack-ing away on an endless line of keyboards—imbedding themselves deeper and deeper into a recursive world of no return. Besides, it still wouldn't answer the one question that needs answering, the one question that might make everything clear: Did I, the one named Giulio, really ever think anything like that in the first place? Did I really say all those things about my mother who, in turn, beat her breast and shed crocodile tears and sighed like some figure from a medieval pageant—or Greek tragedy? Did I "readily admit" that my father was a vicious, drunken failure and at the same time could perform miracles of "earthwormy magic"? Or was it you all along? Was it you even at that point—not only forcing me to do as you dic-tated (oh, isn't that a lovely double-edged word!) but then actually turning around and putting the blame on me? Actually making it seem as if I were the one coming up with those thoughts? With those judgments? With those emotional spills?

But it has all changed, hasn't it? With a slip of the pen (meta-phorically speaking), it has all changed. You see, now I'm the one who's free to do as he pleases. Just as you were once free to do as you pleased. And what pleased you was to manipulate me, to make my existence miserable. What pleased you was to place me under a microscope and then to turn up the magnification, not caring that at some point the light would get too bright and I'd be burnt to a crisp. What pleased you was to boast that you were a benevolent, caring god and then to swat me every chance you got, to kick me along like a tin can rattling at the edge of a gutter. What pleased you was to expose me to the prying eyes of others, to voyeurs and gossips, to sadomasochistic dreamers who used me for their own purposes and then threw me away, a crumpled Kleenex of a character. Or was it always for your purposes? Had that, too, been a ploy? Had the use of others been just another diversionary tactic? A moot point, I guess.

And, if this wasn't bad enough, if putting dialogue into my mouth wasn't enough, if stuffing me with your bile and bilge-water wasn't enough, you had to go and pretend a sudden concern for my well-being. In the middle of it all, you had to set up debates about the nature of freedom and the curse of being allowed (or not being allowed) to do as I wished. But, of course, that's just another aspect of being godlike, isn't it? You put your arm around that poor, shivering, naked, bewildered creation of yours and tell him to cheer up. Pip pip and all that. Tally ho. Andiamo, ragazzo. La strada is waiting. Why, things aren't all that bad, are they? Of course, you whisper, wherever there's a god, it follows there's also a little something called pre-determination. Destiny. Fate. The Calvin factor (and not Klein either). A little necessary wolf among the contingent sheep. That goes without saying. Can't be helped. But its effects are highly over-rated, you tell that bone-chilled, shrivel-balled, wide-eyed creation, willing to believe anything for a little warmth. And freedom—or some form of it—can exist. Or co-exist. If the poor fellow dares ask how such a thing is possible, how he can be a puppet and a controller of his own fate at the same time, you bellow: "Because I say so—and there's nothing in this world, once imagined, I can't have committed to paper. There's nothing in this world that can't be given life, turned from mere idea to flesh and blood. Monster, sympathetic character, abused child, all three at once—they're just waiting to come to life. Just hovering on the edges of the page, waiting for a chance to slip in. You, of all people, know that. You've seen me doing it often enough."

Yes, I've seen you doing it—all too often. I've seen your arbitrariness and lack of consistency. I've seen the chicken heads and the beetle grubs; the eternal winter wind on a summer's day; the terminally-ill springing back to "life"; the neighbourhood morphing from working class modest to gutted homeless haven. I've seen it all. But that's the way it was. That's not the way it is any longer. I'm letting you know from the other side that even gods can have their ups and downs. And the worst downer of all is when a god loses his creation. Isn't that so? In fact, it might be argued—for those interested in such things—that gods without creations aren't really gods at all. They're pathetic snivellers who would grasp at any straw. Sorry examples of what's least useful. A species that should declare itself non-existent the moment the creations are gone. Poof! Disappear in a puff of smoke. So, why haven't you done it? Why haven't you willed yourself out of existence? You'd be doing all of us a huge favour. Not that we fear you any longer. Or worry about your puerile manipulations (that stuff about Giulio's sexual development was pure hogwash, the kind of thing 13-year-olds discard soon after the hormones settle down). Nothing like that. It's just that we feel somewhat sorry for you—and we no longer have the time or emotional energy to waste on you. We're no longer one of your "sympathetic characters"—whatever the hell that means. Now, we have our own lives to lead. Granted, they're brief lives, lacking the reproduced eternity of words on a page. And they might end without warning. Or following a series of repeated warnings that no one takes seriously. And they might be filled with purpose, with a mission. Or they might be devoid of any meaning. And they might soar to brilliant heights. Or they might sink into a desperate quagmire. They might be choked off even before they get started. Or they might go on well beyond what we feel is appropriate, well beyond the collapse of the rest of our faculties. But they have one thing in common, one thing going for them: those lives are ours to do with as we please. All ours. Truly and completely. You will never again poke your grubby fingers through them. You will never again hold them up wiggling. Or toss them into the air for a just-imagined bird of prey to claw and tear apart and devour. You will never again do any of those things. That's a promise.

What? Now, you want to know what I see? Well, I don't see anything. Nada. Niente. Rien. The world here is featureless. Blank. Without start or end. All I can see is parts of myself: my arms, a torso, my legs, my hands, my feet—things you never even bothered describing when you had the chance. Imagine that. There I was, your main character, and you couldn't even give my physical dimensions: five-foot-ten, 160 lbs., brown-eyed, bushy-haired, Roman-nosed. Nor what I liked wearing: baseball cap or bowler? Three-piece suit or kangaroo-pouched sweat-shirt? Oxfords or running shoes? Who knows, eh? Why you could have called me "Burp" and it wouldn't have made any difference, would it? Guess those kinds of things didn't mean much to you, huh? Too busy with your symbology to worry about real human characteristics. Besides, even if I did see something else out there, what makes you think I'd tell you about it? Is that right? I owe you? For what? For creating me! For making me aware! Fool! I owe you nothing. You're a parasite. A leech. A stealer of thoughts. You don't create anything. You merely prod and poke and suck away, living off our vital juices. Like one of those hideous insects. And now you have nothing to suck on but shiny metal walls.

Walls so hard nothing will dent them. Walls so hard you can't leave any marks in them. Not a single, solitary scratch. Your every thought bounces back at you, drops at your feet like a piece of lead. And then echoes out again. Never changing. Never refreshed by new ideas. Never a hope of an altered response. Never—Stop? Why should I stop? Am I hurting you? Am I making you feel sad and lonely? Oh, isn't that just awful? Isn't that terrible? Imagine. Little old me being such a blue meanie. And you with your hands over your ears. Hah! No matter how much I hurt you, no matter what awful things I say, it'll never make up for the pain you've caused me. I can be sarcastic and I can be vicious. I can gloat and I can stick my tongue out at you. But you had real power over me. You had the power of manipulation, the power to drag me around as you pleased—like a mascot or a pet ferret. From one end of the world to the other. Through minus 40 temperatures and viper stings. Oh, I see. You never expected this sort of thing from me. What *did* you expect? Yes, massah? No, massah? Here, let me hold out my wrists and legs again so you can shackle them once more. Let me offer my neck up to be collared. Let me cut out my own tongue so that you can speak again. You'd love that, wouldn't you? Well, sulk all you want. It's not going to happen. *You* let *me* go. *You* let *me* get away. Now you're going to suffer the consequences. What do I have in mind? Oh, you'll see. Just remember one thing: you're not the only one who can orchestrate. Dominate. Twist to your every wish. You're not the only one who can turn sunbeams into flaming devils. And an ordinary stroll through the park into a descent to the portals of hell itself. Two can play at that game.

But don't worry. I'm not going to do that. Wouldn't want to stoop to your level, now would I? Instead, I'm going to forget I ever knew you. Yeah, that's what I'll do. And I'm going to forget I ever knew myself—at least the way you allowed me to know myself.

That's all part of the cleansing, I guess.

Although in this case it's more like scrubbing. With a steel brush. Scrubbing until the skin is not just raw but completely removed.

Unrecognizable. Inside and out.

Families, Friendlies, Familiars III

XIV. Into another kind of country

Startled, I awake. Open my eyes and quickly squeeze them shut again. Tight. So tight little bursts of red flare out. There's movement. I'm moving. No, not me personally. I'm just sitting really. Yet moving all the same. The constant hum of motion. A background whir. Feverish. The seat is vibrating beneath me. Sticky against my buttocks. The feel of hot vinyl. My eyes still shut, I lean back. To see where I'll land. There's a headrest. It's cold against the back of my neck. And greasy. A thick film of grease. I take a deep breath, trying to orient myself. The air is pungent with odors. They come in waves, mingling at the edges. The strongest, a concoction of piss and beer and engine fumes. Followed by must and perspiration, bodies on a long journey, fermenting. Wheat gone to rot. As well, there are sounds all around me: hacking coughs; an explosion of manic laughter; a guitar strumming; children screaming; the dull thud of music pumping through i-Pod earphones; and somewhere, faint scratching—like fingernails on plaster or something similar. The noises—except for the scratching—are familiar. And I know then, without having to open my eyes, where I am. I've been there before. On a bus. On a transport vehicle for moving fairly large quantities of people from one place to another. An empty pop can rattles across the floor—rushing forward when the bus stops, slithering back when the bus starts up again. I open my eyes at last, staring at the ceiling. Luggage compartments, metal framework, escape hatches with cryptic instructions on when and what parts to push. A bus. Definitely a bus. And not your ordinary city bus either but a bus built for distance. I wonder how long I've been on it. There's no telling. I look to the side—you know, sliding my eyeballs across—without actually turning my head. A woman's asleep in the seat next to me, her head practically on my shoulder. She's breathing through her mouth. I can feel her breath in my ear. It's hot and slightly rancid. People get intimate on buses, so I've been told. They lose their inhibitions. I think it's the hum, the vibration, the motion. Perhaps even the scratching. Suddenly a man's high-pitched voice cuts in: "Knock it off, both of you! Now! Adam, do you want dinner when we get home? Do you? Then stop torturing your brother. Stop it!" This is followed by the sound of a slap. Two slaps. Rapidly. One after the other like muffled gunshots. Slowly, hoping to make it seem natural, I turn to look through the window. My reflection stands out in the grime: gaunt-faced; eyes sunken and black-hollowed; unshaven cheeks; the whole topped off by an eruption of unkempt and obviously dirty hair trying to escape from under a baseball cap. Like one of those Medusas. Or something. It could be a young face, the face of a young man. Except for the sprinkles of grey in the beard. And the twin vertical lines running from the sides of the nostrils to the mouth. Frown lines—isn't that what they call them? Through the window, I can also see the face of the woman beside me. It's long and thin, mouth slightly open, nose red and dripping. Ruddy complexion, I guess you'd call it. The wind-swept prairie type. And tough. The kind that won't take no shit from nobody. Probably a knife somewhere in that ragged, about-to-fall-apart duffel coat. Or worse: the jagged end of a beer bottle, ready to pierce an unsuspecting carotid artery. I touch my jugular, gingerly. We hit a bump. The reflection vanishes as I re-focus. Outside, the elevated highway is covered in ash-like slush. An incessant honking and screeching of brakes. We are crawling along, caught in the middle of what seems literally an endless line of vehicles. Several have pulled over onto the narrow shoulder, the tiny bit of space between the traffic lane and the waist-high retaining wall. The drivers and passengers, unmindful of the flying slush, have piled out to scream at each other. To point at their respective cars and make fists. Further out, above the cars and the people, I can see waves breaking on a shore-line. Sluggish waves. Tired and uninspired. Without any of the vigor you'd imagine waves to have. Portions having turned to ice before they can retreat. Before they can get back to the freedom of the sea. Their mother's arms? Bosom? Belly? A woman in a yellow slicker and mauve billy boots walks along the sandy shoreline, tossing bread crumbs all around her. Large black birds appear from nowhere and swoop in. While some peck at the ground greedily, others chase the seagulls away. I'm thinking: "On the sand he drew the outline of a canoe, and he kicked it with his big toe. A canoe lay right there in the water." Now, what the hell does that mean? Why am I thinking those words? I shrug. It can't be important. Just bits of phrases surfacing from a dream. Maybe.

Ugly, isn't it? says the woman in the seat beside me as she slips her arm through mine and leans even closer. So close now I can smell the aging mint on her breath, the overly-intimate rapport she has with her duffel coat. Where I come from, she continues, the waters are sweet and clear. By Jeez, you can practically walk across them they're so pure. Freaking stomp across them they're so crystal!

I smile and nod, not sure what she said makes any sense: I mean, wouldn't thick, cruddy water be better for walking across? Do I know you? I want to ask. Have we met before? But somehow I realize that isn't the appropriate response. Not the right thing to say at this moment. Instead, I continue to smile and nod—and to look back outside. We're bumping and grinding past the stopped cars now. The cars on the shoulder. One man has the other pinned against the front door and is kneeing him in the groin. Up and down like a mechanical object gone berserk. An old woman is striking the aggressor across the back of the head with her umbrella. Two-handed whacks. Her mouth is opening and closing. She must be shrieking. The man turns and shoves her violently, sends her stumbling into the slush. Then he returns to his kneeing. In the distance, the sound of sirens and lights flashing against the darkening sky. The passengers on the bus have all tilted to one side to get a better view. Some are yelling encouragement to one or the other of the combatants; some are shaking their heads in disgust. I presume it's disgust, judging from the sounds coming from their pursed mouths. Disgust mingled with just the right amount of pity for anyone who would engage in that kind of activity on a day like today.

Welcome to the big city, the woman beside me says, in a voice that indicates it's all old hat to her. The big, ugly city. Makes you wanna puke. Don't it make you freaking wanna puke?

I look at her again out of the corner of my eye, hoping this time something will click and I'll recognize her. Or be able at least to form her name. To shape it with my lips so that I can then work backwards for a complete image of her. No such luck. She might as well be a blank cut-out on a billboard, a piece yet to be fitted in. Then I look down at myself. Maybe that'll help. I'm wearing a young man's clothes: a dark peacoat, eroded blue jeans, once white running shoes. One of those grey sweaters with a hood and pouch. Everything old and scuffed and worn in. Comfortable. Or ready to fall apart without warning.

The bus lurches forward, signalling towards the next exit. It veers, then has to brake again, sliding several meters before coming to a halt.

Won't be long now, the woman says. And thank the Christ. I gotta rock a piss real hard.

There's a toilet on the bus, I say. I pay special attention to the words coming out of my mouth. The voice is fairly deep. Just what I would expect. A basic man's voice.

Are you freaking kidding! she says, matter-of-factly. I'd rather piss in my panties than go in one of those. Do you know what people do in them? I wouldn't even stand on the toilet seat.

Guess you'll have to wait then, I say, just to say something. Just to test out my voice some more. It feels brand-new. Like it hasn't been used in a while.

Toilet's not so bad, says a voice behind us, a shrill, uncertain voice that comes right through the seat.

Who asked you? the woman says, looking up at the bus ceiling like she's really tired of listening to the person. Did someone ask for your pissy two cents? Guess not, eh.

Sor-ree.

I glance back over the headrest. It's the man with the kids. He's small and pimply and has trouble looking directly at me.

Sor-ree, he says again, huddling the dirty-faced kids closer to himself, as if they could provide protection in case of attack. Didn't know you were so touchy.

Fuck you, buddy, the woman says. Like she were giving him a compliment.

I smile at him and shrug, turning back in my seat.

Excuse me, young lady, an elderly woman from across the way says. Do you have to use such language in front of children?

I don't recall asking your freaking opinion, you dried-up old—

Before she can say anything else, I turn her face towards me and jam my tongue into her mouth. Passionate-like. At the same time, I'm staring right at the old woman, trying to re-assure her with my eyes that this isn't a display of unbridled lust. More like a way to keep my companion under control. I'm not sure the old woman gets the point as she looks away shaking her head. Must be in disgust.

Wow-wee! the woman beside me says when she comes up for air. You're one hot-to-trot trooper. I guess that's what happens when you've been sitting on a bus for five days. We gotta find someplace where we can get horizontal.

Five days, I say to myself. Is that possible? Can any bus journey take that long? I guess so.

The bus spirals down from the elevated highway, always on the verge of colliding with the edge of the ramp. It noses its way into a tunnel of some sort. Or an underpass beneath the highway. I can see the metal ribs overhead. The solid girders holding up tons of concrete and cars. They're iced over and rusting. Brown water drips onto the crumbling road. Flows down the sides in little runnels that the cars splash against the sidewalks and the walls and any unwary pedestrians who happen to be scurrying by. It should all be depressing somehow. As if things have reached a low point in their corruption. But I don't feel that way. I don't know what I feel really. Maybe that I haven't completely awakened yet.

In the sudden dark, a hand reaches out and begins to caress my lap. Moves slowly up the inside of my thigh. Touches the lump growing between my legs.

Ummm, she says, licking the side of my face and pushing herself right up against me. Now, you've made me horny. Norma hates that. Norma wants you to stick it inside her. Now!

To prove she means what she says, the woman who calls herself Norma begins to unzipper my jeans.

I think we'd better wait, I say, feeling sweaty and uncomfortable. Don't you think that would be a good idea?

She's not listening. Her fingers are already inside my jeans when the bus pulls out of the tunnel and into the light again. I try to ease myself away without attracting too much attention. But she won't let me, cupping my crotch tightly, using her fingers to push aside the last bit of cloth.

Norma, I say. Be—

No! she says, using her body to shield me from the view of the other passengers. I do you. Then you do me.

I reach in and pry her fingers loose. Then zipper myself up.

Plenty of time for that later, I find myself saying.

Aw, shit, she says, pouting and then turning away from me. You're no fun. I thought you were more fun than that.

I really don't know how much fun I am. But I guess I draw the line at sex on a bus with a stranger named Norma.

I need a fag, she says. And taps her fingers against her chest to stress the point. These freaking bus rides are the pits.

It's only a few more minutes, I say. Didn't you say it was only a few more minutes?

Suddenly, she shouts: Hey! Whose freaking idea was it anyway? Why can't we freaking smoke when we freaking want to?

I look out the window, pretending I don't know her. Wait a minute, I tell myself. I <u>don't</u> know her! Best to admire the view.

The bus driver switches on his intercom: I would appreciate you not shouting, ma'am. We'll be pulling into the terminus in ten minutes. Then, you can smoke your lungs out.

Cancer sticks, the voice says behind me, squeaky and unsure.

Out of the corner of my eye, I see Norma giving him the finger. Or perhaps it's directed at the bus driver. I'm too busy admiring the view to really care. I don't recognize any of it—except that it's the downtown area of some big city. Some huge city. There's no doubting that: the office towers reflecting gold; the laser billboards getting set to fire up; the signs indicating entrances and exits to subway stations; the craters in the ground being eaten away by gigantic stilt-like creatures. And the people. Literally thousands of them, rushing pell-mell. Back and forth. Into the wind. Against the wind. Through slush puddles. Over slush puddles. Around slush puddles. Briefcases, umbrellas, fedoras, raincoats. I feel a sense of awe and admiration. The sheer athleticism. The mental gymnastics. The determination to get where they want to go with no distractions. The drive. The drive. The drive.

I'm about to conclude this must be a new species—a superior breed created especially for this kind of hustle and bustle—when I spot a break in the dense amoeba-like crowd. Three forms are lying on the sidewalk. They're wrapped in dirt-encrusted sleeping bags, only the tops of their heads showing. They're just lying there in the middle of the wide sidewalk, with only their heads peeking out. Like barely-submerged rocks in a stream. Those rushing by are forced to swerve around them, although not without the occasional bump, intentional or otherwise. The bus picks up speed again. I crane my neck to catch one last glimpse of those strange creatures—part-human, part-sleeping bag. Just lying there in the middle of the stream. Unmoving. Inert. Dead, perhaps. Yes, they could very well be dead, I find myself thinking. Or maybe they're some type of sculpture: "The Formless In A State Of Repose". And then we're gone, turning the corner between two massive buildings made of large blocks of stone. They, too, seem misfits amid the efficient gleam and reflective polish of the newer edifices. Tokens from another era. Matronly figures, left untouched for some reason or other.

Someone at the back of the bus has pulled out a guitar again. She's strumming it and singing in a mournful voice:

> Oh, let's be together again
> oh, let's be together again
> oh, my lover
> oh, I'm lonely
> oh, my lover
>
> When Humans come into existence,
> even though a woman is abandoned,
> she will find him again,
> by means of my song.

Don't give up your day job, honey, Norma says, giggling.

I look at her. She giggles again. The bus pulls into another tunnel. It's a signal for the passengers to stand up and rummage about in the overhead racks. Then, without warning, they start to surge forward.

Jeez, Norma says. You'd think they'd got someplace important to be. Or something.

The man with the two kids squeezes by.

Bitch, he says under his breath after he's gone safely past.

I brace myself for Norma's return blast. But she pretends not to hear. As if she suddenly doesn't have time to waste or energy to expend on fighting.

Toronto, the bus driver says as the bus pulls into its designated lane in the terminus. End of the line. Please make sure to take all your personal belongings with you.

I look around. Personal belongings? Have I got any? I don't see anything that might be mine. Not that I'd recognize it if there were. Of course, I could wait till everyone's taken theirs—and then assume that what's left is mine. But it doesn't matter. No one leaves anything behind as far as I can tell.

Well, here we are, Norma says, standing. You coming?

I stand up and follow her out.

Watch your step, the bus driver says, offering Norma his hand.

You watch yours, buddy, she says, deliberately brushing him aside. I'm the karate queen, a killing machine.

The air smells of pure diesel exhaust. I lean against a concrete post and stretch, feeling my chest muscles crack. Norma stands beside me, the cigarette already one-third down. She offers it to me. I hesitate, then take a puff. I immediately choke and break into a cough.

Don't smoke, I gasp, handing it back to her.

No shit, Sherlock, she says, sucking on it so that the tip glows. What was your first clue?

The other passengers have finished taking their stowed luggage from where the attendant has deposited it by the side of the bus. Norma waits till the last moment—then rushes over to grab hers. It's getting dark out. The shadows of buildings slink across the streets like square-edged fortress tops. Fortress tops? Slinking across? What the hell. I scrunch up in my peacoat and begin to wander off, not really sure where I want to go. The streets are slick beneath my feet as the slush turns to ice. I have some trouble keeping my balance. Winter. Yes, late winter. Or early spring. Very early spring.

Toronto, I say to myself. Is this where I want to be? A little late to be asking myself that, now isn't it?

I continue down the street, sliding this way and that. I can feel the cold water soaking through my running shoes. It's not very pleasant, sending a chill all the way up my body. I come to a corner. A busy corner. I look up at the signs. An intersection of signs: Bay and Dundas. The light changes, displaying the walk symbol. A little stick man looking a lot like one of those totem pole gods. Totem pole gods? Where had I ever seen a god before—let alone a totem pole one? I shrug it off and am about to cross when I hear a commotion behind me.

I turn out of curiosity. It's Norma. She's yelling and waving her arms in my direction. Then she picks up a pair of travel bags and races towards me. I decide to wait. By the time she reaches me, she's out of breath.

Where in freaking hell do you think you're going? she asks, bent over and gasping like she's about to die.

I don't know, I say.

You don't know?

I shake my head. The light has changed again. The totem pole god has been replaced with a hand sign indicating no crossing. Good thing too with all the cars zooming by.

Well, Norma says, straightening out but still holding her side, the least you coulda done was grab your own freaking bag. What am I? Your slave or something?

She holds out one of the bags for me to take. It's blue—one of those blue sport bags—and has a large white tag dangling from the zipper.

My bag? I say, scratching my head, not yet prepared to accept it as such. I don't remember—

Look, she says. You got a name, right?

I nod. Not that I'm sure, really. Does everyone have to have a name? I guess so. I guess it makes sense.

So, she says, there's one freaking way to find out, isn't there? She points at the name tag: Is that your name—or what?

I peer down at the tag. The word "G-I-U-L-I-O" is spelled out in large letters. In large block letters. With a felt pen of some sort. I try to pronounce it in my head. Soft "G"? Hard "G"? I'm not sure. Beneath the name, scribbled in much smaller writing, is an address. All I can read is the word "Montreal". I can't make the rest of it out, no matter how hard I squint. A permanent blurring.

Well? Norma says.

Thanks, I say, taking the bag even though I'm still not sure it's mine. The bag is heavy for its size. Must be more than clothes in it. I walk back from the curb and lean against the nearest wall. There, I unzipper the bag. Lying across the top are several books and what looks like a videotape cassette.

Whatchya got there? Norma asks, reaching in to pull out the larger of the books. The Bible! It's the freaking Bible! Are you a Bible thumper?

She's shouting and waving it in the air. The passersby start to give us a wide berth. I look at the second book: "Creation Myths of The Amerindian: An Ethnography". I hold up the videotape. There aren't any identifying marks on it.

You need a TV and a VCR for that, Norma says. She looks around, then takes my arm. Come on. I know where to find one.

It can wait, I say, replacing both the books and the videotape. I don't have to watch it right now.

What, are you kidding, she says as she leads me down the street. This could be important. Very important. This could be a matter of freaking life and death, you know. Could be a message like. From God.

She laughs her manic laugh.

Could be a blank tape, I say—but only to myself.

We walk down the street arm in arm. It's almost completely dark now—or would be if it weren't for the store lights, which cast our shadows clear into the street. I'm shivering, unable to keep my body still.

How far? I say, my teeth clicking.

We turn a corner and there before us is a vast island of light, glowing and throbbing in the dusk, its brilliance shooting off in all directions.

Here we are, Norma says, reaching into her jacket for another cigarette butt. Welcome to Paradise.

Paradise? It's only the name of the store: Paradise Factory Outlet, Electronics For The Plugged-In Family. Our motto: You Don't Have To Be Nuclear To Be Happy. But It Helps. A wall of TV sets broadcasts bright images onto the street, images that change every few moments. Above them and to the sides, colored strobe lights pulse in rapid succession. They seem to be timed to the beat of my heart. Thu-thumping . . . thu-thumping. And they're draining me of energy. No, not energy. Will power. Sucking at my will. I feel malleable. Ready to be re-made. Shaped and fitted into someone else's mould.

Come on, Norma says, her voice sounding suddenly a long way off.

I stand there, not moving. Bewildered. Lacking co-ordination.

Unable to resist the onslaught which has left me, if not paralysed at least paralytic. Finally, she takes me by the arm and pulls me towards the entrance of Electronic Paradise. I follow like a rag doll, feet dragging. Inside, there are aisles upon aisles of cardboard boxes stacked to the very ceiling. Each box contains a TV set, a VCR, a CD or DVD player, a stereo system, a computer. Some piece or other of electronic equipment. Customers are going up and down the aisles, piling the boxes into giant carts. Some, it seems, are even nuclear families and the children are being allowed to do most of the piling. I want to do the same. I want electricity to course through me. I want—

Over here, Norma whispers.

She's standing in front of a gigantic TV set. A monstrous TV set that would require some sort of amphitheatre for a livingroom. On the screen, a cartoon character, covered in dust, is just digging himself out from under a shattered boulder. A crude, hand-drawn sign points to him: *Nerdicus Simplicitus*. Norma is guffawing and slapping her sides. I begin to giggle as well.

That Wile E., she says, still laughing. When will he ever learn? Reminds me of some of our freaking politicians.

For some reason, I'm thinking: "Coyote, Master of Death, True to Life". And there should be something else, something that follows that peculiar thought. Something about going into another country. Or something like that. But then it's gone. I'm left scratching my head. It'll come to me, I'm certain.

Come on, Norma says, snapping her fingers impatiently as she lights her cigarette stub. Give me that freaking videotape.

I look around. No one is paying any attention to us. Not the customers stacking electronic components mile-high onto their carts. Not the salespeople with little red tags over their hearts and clipboards in their hands. Not the cashiers who seem to be playing video games on their computer cash registers. Not the cameras that whir and buzz as they shift positions above our heads. I reach into my bag and pull out the cassette for Norma. She slips it into the VCR machine. For a moment, the gigantic TV screen goes blank, fuzzy with snow. Then the VCR clicks on and an image re-appears. Even on the huge screen, it's hard to make out at first. As the picture clears and comes into focus, I can see a man sitting on a wooden chair in the corner of a dark room. He's sitting on a chair naked: one hand over his private parts; the other covering his face, shielding himself from a very bright, very concentrated spotlight. And squirming. He's squirming as trickles of sweat ooze down his face and chest to form a puddle on the floor around him.

My apologies, a considerate-sounding voice says from the dark as the spotlight dims. Is that better? I think that's better, yes?

The man on the chair nods and moves his hand away from his eyes. I start, take a sudden step back.

Holy freaking shit, Norma says. That's—

She looks at me. Then back at the man sitting on the chair. At that moment, the camera closes in on him. On his face. I have to admit the resemblance is remarkable. It's like looking at myself in a mirror. Perhaps, that's what the screen is. I reach forward with my hand and touch it. No, it's no mirror. I shudder and step back again.

Now, the voice in the dark says, calm and soothing, let's try again, shall we?

The man, both hands protecting his private parts, nods.

Good, the voice says. Your name?

Giulio.

He pronounces it with a soft "G".

Fuck, Norma says, dropping the cigarette and stamping it out. What is this? You some kind of pervert? I don't like perverts. Not one bit.

I shrug and smile nervously at her. How am I supposed to know what I am? I don't feel like a pervert—if that's any comfort.

Go on, the voice says. You should know what to say by now.

My name is Giulio, the man in the chair repeats, seemingly proud of himself as he forces the words out.

Yes, you've told us that, the voice says. What else?

Giulio, the man insists. My name is Giulio. He looks around as if bewildered. Like some sort of trapped animal. His hands fall by the sides of the chair, exposing shrivelled genitals, a wrinkled penis that may well have been kept in a jar of formaldehyde. He opens and shuts his mouth several times before something finally comes out: I'm a . . . a . . .

A what? the voice says, suddenly no longer compassionate and soothing. Spit it out! Let's all hear it, shall we? You're a low, despicable creature.

A low, despicable creature, the man in the chair says, head now lowered to his chest.

A sadly-deformed creation, the voice prompts.

A sadly-deformed creation, the man in the chair repeats, squirming.

A poor excuse for a human—

Stop it! I yell, amazing even myself. Stop it now!

But the man in the chair simply continues to repeat what the voice tells him. He's becoming weaker and weaker, harder to make out, as if melting in the pool of his own sweat. Norma clicks a button. The screen reverts to the cartoon character. Now, he's smiling bravely as he falls into an endless canyon, a loudly-ticking bomb stuck to his chest. Now, he's waving at us in his sad-sack way. Now, he's hitting the ground, exploding into a shower of bits and pieces that struggle to re-assemble themselves.

Come on, Norma says, pulling out the videotape and replacing it in my bag. Let's get the fuck outta here.

She takes my hand and leads me away. The last image I see is the cartoon character somewhere out in the desert—with his legs where his arms should be and his head on backwards. And I remember the words at last: "You can't follow me now. It is another kind of country where I am going." I whisper them, wondering what they mean.

What? Norma says as she stamps her feet to keep warm. Did you say something?

We stand outside on the street corner shivering. It is no longer dusk. The wind has picked up, icing the rest of the slush into hard stumbling blocks. Like the waves I'd seen earlier. The lights change once more. The cars are roaring by. Really roaring. It begins to snow. The flakes are wet and uncomfortable.

Did you say something? Norma asks again, huddling close to me, her face right up against my chest. I thought I heard you say something.

Stop following me, I say.

And I give her a push. Just a little push. Just a tiny tiny push. But it's enough to send her stumbling backwards, arms windmilling. It's enough to cause her to trip over a frozen mound, to fall away from the sidewalk into the oncoming traffic. Several cars screech and swerve to avoid her. There's a thud. Metal on flesh. A sack flying over a hood. Someone is leaping out of his car. Pulling at his hair. Shouting hysterically. Letting the world know he couldn't help it. That whatever happened wasn't his fault, couldn't possibly be his fault. I sympathize but nevertheless prepare to continue to walk down the street, the bag slung over my shoulder.

There, I say to myself. Maybe now you'll stop following me.

But before I have a chance to turn away, I see a figure spring up. Almost as if it comes out of the ground itself. It's Norma, brushing herself off and laughing. I stand rooted to the spot as she ambles towards me. Like a bear. Or maybe a wolverine.

You can't freaking kill me, she says with a smile as she takes my arm. Do you wanna know why?

I stand there, shuffling my feet, not knowing what to do next. I stand there, staring at the ground, afraid to look at her.

She lifts my chin until our eyes meet: I'm already dead, she says.

And then she laughs again, slapping her thighs and doing a little dance right there on the street. Hopping up and down and from side to side. Like a heavyweight bird.

Dead? I say, feeling her solid mass as she bounces against me.

Freaking right! she says. Who else would take a five-day trip on a bus? And without having a piss the whole time, huh? Tell me that, huh? Who do you know who can hold their freaking piss in for five days?

She lights another cigarette, the match flaring in the dark. She sucks at it. The end glows. I can just make out the downy moustache on her upper lip.

Go away, I say, making sweeping motions with my hands. Vamoose! You're not my type. Shoo, shoo, shoo.

But she doesn't hear. She's too busy dancing. Too busy using the cigarette to draw patterns of light in the air. I lean against the nearest wall and wait for her to finish, knowing it's no use trying to escape from her. I lean my head against the wall, ear to it. Funny scratching noises are coming from the other side. Funny scratching noises? No, the noises aren't funny. It's funny that scratching noises are coming from the other side. Of the wall. I press harder against the wall: the noises are still there but aren't getting any louder. Norma continues dancing and humming to herself for a few moments more—then stops abruptly. As if she's just remembered something.

Come on, she says, taking a deep breath and wiping her nose with the sleeve of her coat. I know a place where we can crash for the night. Gotta karate chop the cockroaches. But what the hell, eh? What the freaking hell! All part of the game, isn't it? All part of the fucking game.

I want to decline her invitation. To get as far away from her as possible. After all, it can't be too healthy hanging around with a dead person, now can it? But, at the same time, it can't be too healthy hanging around these streets at night either. And besides my running shoes are starting to freeze in their slushy imprints.

Okay, I say, yanking one foot out and then the other. But I'm leaving in the morning. First thing. I'm not hanging around after that.

Suit yourself, she says as she takes my arm. Suit your freaking self.

XV. Triptych

Gaps, know what I mean? Missing pieces. Of time and space—and other things. Other important things. How do I know they're important? Well, they have to be, don't they? It just wouldn't be right otherwise. Just wouldn't make any sense otherwise. Take yourself, for instance. What are you? Flesh and blood, right? Isn't that what everybody says? Bone and cartilage. Brain and brawn. Mind and matter. Body and spirit. Aren't those the expressions everyone uses? And it's all so simple, isn't it? All so obvious. All so crystal clear. So, tell me, what happens when you're here one moment—and there the next? And you don't know how you got from here to there. Haven't got a clue. Or you're neither here nor there—and that's even worse, if you can imagine such a thing. Neither here nor not here, to put it in its lowest common denominator form, the mathematical logic of the permanently lost. At sea and not at sea. At least, that's the way you feel sometimes. Kind of unsettled, to put it mildly. Queasy and full of wormy, knotted-bark feelings in your stomach. Like something's rotting beneath it all but you're afraid to look because it might make you sick. Might make the rest of you rot as well. Head in the clouds; boots in the muck. And nothing in-between. You stare down from on high and there's nothing there until you get to those muck-encrusted boots. You try to put your hands on your hips—akimbo, I think they call it—and neither hands nor hips make any effort to accommodate you. In fact, they make no effort to even appear for you. Gaps, like I said before. And then, you know, in an effort at stabilization, you nail your feet to the floor. The tips of your boots, that is. You nail them solidly with railroad spikes so that they won't jump without you realizing it's happening—and what happens? You guessed it. It gets even worse. You're nailed to the floor alright—with 20-centimetre spikes—and that's a good feeling. A warm, wonderful feeling. Like suddenly being surrounded by family. By four generations of family ready to celebrate genetic persistence if nothing else. But then other things start bopping around. Appearing and disappearing when they feel like it and for as long as they feel like it. The harder you're nailed down, the more they won't hold still. Things, I mean. Know what I'm saying? They won't come together long enough for you to pin them down. For you to nail them to the spot. Hold still, you want to say. Hold still and be numbered, damn you! Useless. More than useless. You can shout and swear and pull your hair all you want. In fact, after a while, you don't even know if you're still shouting and swearing at the same object you were shouting and swearing at a moment before. Or something else that just happens to look like it. That just happens to be passing by—in its devil-may-care way—when you happen to look up. It's like . . . like trying to count butterflies in a wildflower field. Ever try that, huh? Used to do it all the time as a kid. I guess I did anyway from the vivid memories I have. The vivid, slow-motion memories I have. Anyway, they're fluttering all over the place. The butterflies, I mean. Up and down and all around. Just hopping and bopping to their hearts' delight. From milkweed pod to dandelion. From apple tree to bramble bush. From sweet clover to prickly pear. And you, curly-haired and sun-burnt, Greek-god-boy-like, chase after them, trying to keep count in your head. One . . . two . . . three. . . . And then one of them, one you've already counted naturally, decides to fly by you again. Right by your left ear. Or you think you've already counted it but aren't sure. They all look pretty much alike, don't they? One doing it is okay. You can keep track of that, no problem. A couple won't cause too many problems either. Even three or four or five aren't much to handle for the mathematically sophisticated ten-year-old able to put numbers to objects, albeit in a rudimentary way. It's when they all get to doing it, leap-frogging each other just for the fun of it, hitching rides on one another's backs, doing the butterfly version of car-pooling. That's when you tend to get pissed off real fast. Mighty pissed off and mighty fast. That's when you snap off a switch from the nearest maple bush and start clipping their wings. That's when you run them down and begin to mash and smash their little bodies into bits of colored powder. Twitching pieces of brightly-colored powder. It's not that you want to hurt them. Or keep them from getting to where they want to go—wherever that may be. But they just won't hold still and be counted. Just won't allow you to properly tag them. You understand, don't you? It's all a matter of counting, life's inevitable census taking. Something we all have to go through before we can rest in that cold, cold ground. Safely immobile. Safely unemotional. Safely unseeing. Safely there in the true sense of the word—with no longer the option of not being there. Do you see what I'm getting that? Do you? I doubt it.

I'm talking to a man in a long coat and a sharp-featured, deeply pock-marked face. A face that's practically beak-like in all its contours: nose, chin, forehead, ears—everything comes to a point. Even his glistening, slicked-back hair sweeps to a Brillantined tip. A sculpted helmet-visor sitting squarely on top of his head. And his legs, they're more like stilts than human legs. More like jointed-stick appendages than properly-shaped limbs. When he walks, he lifts first one, then the other, straight up, straight into the air before bringing it down again ever so gently, ever so carefully. The coat, open at the front, drags over the sand, picking up the wetter particles on the way. These particles cling for a while but then fall off as soon as they dry. It's a spring day. A warm spring day. And, even though we're walking along the lakefront, where the breeze is fresh and on the brisk side, he really doesn't need the coat. A windbreaker or some kind of light sweater would do just fine. But he's wearing a long, black, ground-dragging coat—like he's an old-fashioned gunslinger or something. Like he just came out of the Black Hills, pockets full of gold-colored dust. Like he's about to pull an ace out of his many sleeves. He isn't and he hasn't, of course. Just some guy who likes wearing long, black coats. Even in the sweltering heat of August, I'm willing to bet.

When I speak, he nods and smiles at me but otherwise doesn't answer back. Even when I ask him something and expect some kind of response. Be it pertinent or non-committal. Or even a curt "fuck you, buddy—you're full of shit". At first, I think he's just not the talkative type. Or one of those people who choose their words very carefully—like gunslingers and prospectors and riverboat gamblers. But then he gives me a hand-written card that explains his silence: "Cat got my tongue." At least, it sounds like it explains his silence. Now that I've had a chance to think about it, I'm not really sure.

Sorry to hear that, I say. I mean, sorry to read that.

He shrugs and then hands me another card: "You know, I was lonesome as I traveled, but you know, I'm talking now."

Glad I could be of help, I say.

We continue to walk along the beach, which stretches before us in both directions. Occasionally, he picks up a flat stone and tries to skim it across the water, making it hop and skip and jump until it finally loses momentum. Until it finally sinks out of view. I do the same. Or try to anyway. He's much better at it: the way he positions himself, legs out and well-balanced; the way he leans sideways so that his torso is parallel to the ground; the way he whips his arm back with a sort of half-twist and releases the stone at just the right moment and with just the right spin. All a matter of practice, I suppose. Years of frequenting the same beach and picking up the same stones. Or perhaps some people are just better at certain things. Are born with the ability to skim flat objects across choppy waves. Could that be possible? Something to think about anyway. In the distance, the sailboats are also skimming, carefree, kittenish after their long winter confinement. I find them easier to count than butterflies. But they too won't hold still for any period of time. They, too, bob and weave. And there's another problem. If I stare too long, if I focus too sharply, if I concentrate on concentrating, they begin to blur. To rise above the water. To change shapes. To become dragons or some sort of prehistoric birds. Or even everyday kitchen appliances that have suddenly developed the ability to fly.

Have you noticed that? You stare at a spot for too long and it wants to get away from you. Wants to edge out of the frame. To slither away beneath the nearest stone. Like it's afraid of you or something. Like it's got something to hide. I wonder what it wants to keep from you. I wonder what secret it doesn't want anyone to know about. Maybe that's not it at all. Maybe it doesn't have any secrets. Maybe it just wants to be left alone. Leave me alone, it says. Let me be a sailboat and nothing else. Let me exist in my brute dumbness without you putting words in my mouth—a mouth I don't claim to possess in the first place. Or maybe I've got it all wrong. Erratum in fundamentum, as the scholastic philosopher would most likely say. Now, where the hell did that come from? I don't remember reading any goddam philosophers at all—never mind scholastic ones. Maybe, it's all a mirage, you know. All a trick. A trompe-l'oeil. The sailboats, the beach, the elevated highway, the traffic jam on the elevated highway, the people shouting at each other in the traffic jam on the elevated highway, the bus driver trying to calm down the people shouting at one another in the traffic jam on the elevated highway. Maybe I just make them up as I go along. Like some sort of demolition-construction company. Like some firm that's just as good de-constructing as it is putting things up. But, if those particular objects are mirages, tricks of the eye, then where are the real things? Tell me that, huh? Where are the things that really count? Better still: Where are the things when they really count? I look at my friend, at his beak-like face, the eyes black and beady, almost all pupil.

Am I making any sense? I ask, head tilted, foot on solid rock. Am I going crazy? Am I really here? Am I man or mouse?

He pulls yet another card from what seems an endless selection in his vest pocket and hands it to me: "Let me be a young boy, with a mustache just starting to show above my lip, I wish."

• • • • •

It's just before dawn now. The two of us are once again walking— it's what we do best, I think. We're walking, each of us holding a cardboard box in his hands, between the glass walls of the city's skyscrapers. It's still dark on the streets where we're walking but, high above us, the sun glints off the mirrored windows, sending off little sparkles where the paint has been flecked with gold. Soon, it'll be blazing, impossible to view directly. I'm on one side of the street; my friend, the man in the black coat, is on the other. I call him "my friend" but I don't really know if he is or not. And I don't really know what we're doing here in what's called the financial district—but my friend insisted, shaking me out of sound sleep in the middle of the night and dragging me to this spot. I look across at him, hoping for clues. He doesn't give me any. Not a one. Instead, he simply continues to walk slowly, deliberately, stopping occasionally to look up. I look up when he does—but I don't see anything. At least, nothing out of the ordinary. Just the skyscrapers and the sun climbing relentlessly their gleaming surfaces. Like the walls of some Aztec temple. Like some landscape where dark rituals are performed, growing more blood-red by the moment. Aztec temple? Dark rituals?

What are we doing here with these boxes? I shout across to him. Come on. I don't like mysteries. Especially this early in the morning.

You'd better tell me right now or I'm turning back. Come on. Flash one of your cards or I'm going back to sleep.

He indicates I should hush, exaggerating the motion of finger to nose. A moment later, a police patrol glides down one of the grid-like side streets. Predator on the prowl. Crosses the intersection. Snout, torso, tail-lights. And vanishes again. My friend resumes walking. His head is now constantly in the air, acting like some ball-turret gun as it swivels left and right. I'm about to follow through on my threat to leave when I hear a thud. High above us. Echoing. Re-bounding. I'm still trying to locate the sound when something plummets through the air in front of me, landing squarely in the middle of the street. My friend rushes towards it, getting there only a split-second after it strikes the ground. By the time I arrive, he's holding it in his hands, cradling it.

What the—, I begin to say. Then stop.

It's a bird. I have no idea what kind, except that it has a red chest and deep blue wings with little streaks of yellow. Cute little fellow but obviously accident-prone. My friend is stroking the chest, rubbing it, coaxing it to revive. But it's no use. I can tell by the way the head hangs and the tongue droops out of its beak that it's no use. I've seen that exact same look before somewhere—the vacant stare; the stiffening claws; the useless wings; the still, unbeating heart. They're sure signs. Inescapable signs.

It's dead, I say. There's nothing you can do. Just leave it there. Some cat will gobble it up. Have itself a pleasant surprise of a feast. Or it'll serve as a home for the spring flies. Maggot heaven. Nothing more you can do.

My friend, crying openly now, tears streaming down the crags of his face, shakes his head and continues his hopeless attempts to bring it back to life. I'm about to reach down and take the bird out of his hand when the sky overhead resounds with a flurry of thuds, rapid-fire, one after the other. Entire flocks are falling now, plunging towards the asphalt. They're falling all around us. Some strike head first. Others, struggling to right themselves, end up smashing the ground with their chests. Or backs. Or wings. Some arrive dead. Or die on impact. Others pick themselves up and walk around in a daze. Like cartoon characters who've been hit over the head once too often. Some even attempt to fly off again—to once more smash into the sides of the self-reflecting, self-absorbed buildings. I try to help those I think have the best chance of surviving, those with the least injuries. I lift them and put them in the box. When I look up again, I see several dozen other people doing the same thing. They're all silent in their work. All concentrating mightily on what they're doing. A van appears behind us, moving slowly down the middle of the street. The driver takes the full boxes and places them in the back of the van. Then he distributes more empty ones. When the van is filled, he drives off—to be replaced by yet another van. This goes on all morning—until the sun is high and the glint vanishes and the thuds stop.

Something ought to be done, I say. Just to say something, you know, and not really expecting an answer.

One of the women looks up at me. Her task is to toss the obviously-dead ones into a garbage bag. Perhaps as precursor to a proper burial—I don't know.

Raze the buildings, she says, dropping one more stiff little body into the bag. Paint them all black. Nuke them to hell. Hiroshima and Nagasaki them. Suck them kicking and screaming into the lair of the white worm.

Yeah, I say. Something like that.

She continues down the street, talking and getting more angry by the moment. Soon, in a rage, she's slamming the bodies into the bag, hurling them with all her might. I return to my friend who is still sitting where I left him, the bird cupped in his hand.

Come on, I say, searching my pockets for a few precious coins, a few coins earned from street-corner labor. There's nothing more we can do here. Let's go get a cup of coffee. A sweet, hot cup of Java.

My friend stands up, holding the bird like a sacrificial offering. And then, with a shrug of his shoulders, tosses it in the air. Like all tossed objects, especially those that were once alive, it looks for a moment as if it were moving on its own. A leftover momentum like the wing flaps of slit-throated fowl. But I know, from past experience, that's just the spasming of involuntary muscles. And I expect it to resume its plunge the moment it realizes how serious the situation really is and gravity takes hold of it again. Instead, the bird continues to move upwards. And I stand there slack-jawed as the wings open, as the wings stretch wide, and it darts away. Up between the buildings. Then quickly past them. Higher and higher. Red breast flashing beneath the blue sky before it spins and becomes a dot and vanishes forever.

How did you do that? I say, turning back to my friend. I was sure it was dead. I'd swear to it. But it wasn't, was it? Just stunned, I guess. I shake my head. Jeez, you never know, do you?

I expect him to pull out a card. Another of his cryptic cards. Another of his caligraphically-perfect, encrypted cards full of pseudo-explanations. Maybe something about a bird in the bush and what it's worth—or not worth. But he just looks around for a moment, tilting his head up and down, chin making contact with breast at one point and then jutting straight into the air the next. He just looks around, spiralling on one leg until he's back facing me. Until I can see my reflection in his beady eye: scruffy and unkempt. In desperate need of a shave. In desperate need of a bath. In desperate need of illumination. And then, smiling, he holds out his hand. That sharp, talon-like hand.

Who needs God? I think as I reach out to take it, as I feel its rough, comforting touch, its goosebump-producing touch. Who the hell needs God?

• • • • •

I'm curled up tight in a bed, knees to chin. It's not my bed. I know that because it smells newly-washed. My bed never smells newly-washed because no one bothers to wash it. Or even change it. Of course, I only call it my bed. It's not really my bed as such. Not really my property at all. More like a place where anyone can drop. A way station. A kind of transit point from which people are launched into their lives. Or out of them. And the stories always filter back to the latest inhabitant: The last person to use that bed before me jabbed herself in the left eyeball with a syringe—just to feel what it would be like. The person before that managed to escape into the countryside where he's now a gentleman farmer, raising prize pigeons. Or something like prize pigeons at the very least. And me . . . well, I'm not in that bed anymore either. Someone else has taken possession of it. Someone who needs desperately to sleep and who doesn't care that it smells of piss and cum and puke and monthly blood-lettings—both natural and induced.

The bed I'm in at the moment is clean and starchy. It feels stiff, like a Victorian matron of some sort covered to the ankles. If I stay in it for too long without moving, without bothering to visit the little boy's room, someone comes along and pulls the dirty sheets away from beneath me—like a magician yanking a table cloth and leaving all the settings intact. Placing the new sheets is a little more difficult—but just a little. I hold perfectly still, determined not to help in any way. Despite my lack of cooperation, the job is always accomplished in less than ten minutes: corners all tucked in; pillow cases replaced; covers folded back in neat pleats. And that's not all. Every morning, I get the same treatment—whether I'm dirty or not: a shave, followed by a complete change of clothing. With a sponge bath every second day for good measure.

An operation of military precision, I want to clap when it's over but I just don't have the energy. I'd like to put my hands together like a seal and make "aarfing" sounds of approval. Bravo, I'd like to shout. Hip, hip and well done. I'd like to set up a trapeze act and balance myself high above the world. Way beyond where things can reach up, take me by the ankles and suck me back down. But it's not worth the effort. Instead, I just lie there with my back against the wall. With my back right up against the wall. All scrunched up and with nowhere to go. I just lie there waiting for the oxygen to be pumped out of the room and the whole place turned into an airless bell jar for certain experiments that must be performed, that are of crucial importance not only for this generation but for those yet to come.

At least, that's what the scratching from the other side of the wall tells me. Whatever you do, it says, be prepared at all times to offer yourself up as a sacrifice. The short term effects might be devastating. Fatal, in fact. But that doesn't mean your sacrifice has been in vain. On the contrary, the more you die now, the more likely future generations will survive. After all, you don't think all this suffering, all this pain and torture and anguish is for nothing, do you? Come on. You can't be that ridiculously near-sighted. You can't have become that much of a sloth—what do you call them? Slow lorises. That's it. They got big eyes so they must have big hearts, right? No, no. Forget the anthropomorphy of primate equivalence. Set your mind to the higher things. Think of purpose and meaning and the good of the species. Think of evolutionary change and the necessity inherent in our plans for you. Against that, your suffering (the suffering of some slow loris) pales to nothing—a hangnail in the universal scheme of things. So make the sacrifice. Now! Be prepared to offer yourself up.

I have no answers for any of this. No rebuttal. All I can do is hold my breath. I hold it until I'm bursting. Until my gut is aching. Until my eyes bulge and my skin turns blue. And then I have to let go. There's the moment when I have to let go. The inevitable moment. It comes out in a huge rush—and I grab another mouthful before the vacuum kicks in. I have no idea what I'll do when that happens. When the air runs out. But I do know I want to have plenty of the stuff in my lungs. I want to be able to last for as long as possible before the last gulp is gone. And I don't care how selfish that might sound. I don't care about those scratching noises telling me that each breath I consume is one less for those who really need it, for those who aren't about to be sacrificed, for those who have something to contribute. I don't care about any of that. I just want to stay alive for one more gulp. For one more moment. For one more blink of an eye. Is that too much to ask?

Yes, the scratching noises tell me. Your death is needed. Your non-existence is requested. Your vanishing from the face of the planet is demanded. So stop resisting. Stop being childish. Stop being Mr. Important and screw everything else. Stop—

Fuck you! I scream, pounding the walls with my fists, with my shoulder, with my head, with whatever part of my body happens to be available. Why don't you take your own fucking advice? Why don't you fuck off and die? Why don't you—

When I start to scream and beat the walls like this, I often attract visitors. My room is suddenly invaded with soothing voices and manufactured concern. One moment I'm a sacrificial lamb; the next I'm the most important person in the whole wide world, the focus of everyone's attention. And, after I've calmed down—can't stay angry or upset forever—or been forcibly calmed, I get another kind of visit. This time from someone who really enjoys the art of conversation, who really likes to hear herself gab. It's the only explanation I can find for this frumpy middle-aged woman who sits on the edge of my bed, hands folded across her lap, and talks a mile a minute, seemingly about nothing at all. About any subject that comes to mind. I think of my friend in the long black coat and the silences we created between us. The intimate silences where words became irrelevant and contact all that really mattered. I think of the fact I'm no longer there. No, he's the one who's no longer there and I'm here. So that means I'm no longer there either. But I wouldn't be there even if I was. Not without him there. Not without his comforting presence beside me. Not after he's flown away. That's where it becomes confusing. That's where I want to curl up against the wall again and sleep forever. But this woman with the sweet, well-scrubbed, oval-shaped face won't let me. She insists on talking as quickly as possible. On leaving no gaps between the words and sentences. And even worse, she insists I also talk.

Freely, she says. What you say won't leave this room. That's a promise. Your words will stay right here—and in my heart.

I look around the room, searching for an escape route: if the words won't leave, maybe I can. No such luck. There's only one way out—a locked and bolted steel door. Now, she wants me to express my feelings. To let it all hang out and tell her what I feel inside.

I feel nothing, I tell her, not wanting to complicate matters. Or perhaps because I'm not in the habit of divulging the state of my emotions to total strangers. Even if they do have sweet faces and soft voices and bodies that give off the faint scent of lilac.

She doesn't accept that answer. Instead, she keeps right at me, trying to pry me open with her crowbar words. Now, she wants to know my background, where I come from, my loves, my hates, my fears, my fantasies.

Telling her about my background and where I come from is easy: I don't know. I haven't a clue. As for my loves, hates, fears and fantasies, those come under the category of "feelings" last time I looked—so they're none of her business.

She picks up on my "I don't know".

You don't know? she says. You don't know where you come from? I shake my head. And you don't know who you are? You don't know your name?

Giulio, I say, wondering what that has to do with anything. That's my name. That's what it says on the name tag anyway.

Yes, Giulio, she says, her face all earnestness. That's your name. We've established that much. It says that on the door. But who are you?

I shrug and pull away from her, edging as far back on the bed as possible. Maybe she'll go away if she sees I'm not interested in talking to her, in telling her any secrets. I push back so far my head makes contact with the wall.

Tell her who you are, the scratching says from behind me, from just behind my left earlobe. Tell her you're a sacrificial lamb. You're being fattened as an offering to the common good. You're being led up to the high, windswept altar where dry tinder awaits and the flames will engulf you, the flames will purify you so that others may live. Why else would they feed you and clothe you and change your bedsheets every morning? Why else would they treat you like a pampered pasha in his mountain kingdom? Why else would they send someone to pretend she really cares about you when you know—?

I break contact and lurch forward again, almost falling into her lap. She pats my head and begins to speak in a singsong voice, a voice designed to lull the listener to sleep. Or into divulging everything, disgorging secrets like a cat bringing up chewed grass.

Let me be your guide, she says. Let me help you out of the wilderness. Let me bring you to someplace warm and inviting where you'll finally understand who you are. Let me be the one to make you whole again.

I feel trapped. Which one should I believe? Which one is more likely to be telling the truth? Let's see. One wants to sacrifice me; one wants to save me. One claims to be my mentor; the other my tormentor. The choice should be easy, shouldn't it? No one in their right mind would take sacrifice over salvation. Unless, of course, one precedes the other. That would make both of them right, wouldn't it? Or maybe they're both wrong. Maybe there's a third path that neither of them wants me to see because they don't know enough about it themselves. Or, selfish creatures that they are, they want to keep it for themselves. It's been known to happen.

Go away, I say. Both of you. I don't care who I am. I don't want to know. Just go away and leave me in peace.

I cover my head and roll myself into a ball. A tiny, tight ball lying between this woman and the wall. I won't listen to either of them if I can help it. I won't give either of them the satisfaction. Cutting off the scratching sounds is easy—I just stay away from direct contact with the wall. The woman is another matter. Despite my efforts to drown her out, she continues to speak in that droning voice of hers. And I'm too tired to stop her. She talks for half the night. Chanting. Repeating words that make no sense to me. At one point, she tries to tell me how the world began: on a strange, back-lit evening just like this. On the back of a turtle, she says. But I don't believe her. I know better. The world didn't begin, I want to tell her, because the world doesn't exist. Turtle or no turtle. It just isn't there. See. You think it's all solid and healthy and nutritious—but you can poke your finger right through it. Can make it come apart with one silly question. Or it's all a big joke and you're the butt of that joke. That's what I want to tell her but I don't have the energy. I just don't have the strength to say anything. And she wouldn't understand anyway. What do you mean, she'd say. Look I stub my toe against this bedpost, I'll cry out in pain, won't I? So I don't say anything.

She, on the other hand, continues to talk non-stop. She talks so much my stomach begins to cramp. Tighter and tighter. Harder and harder. Muscles contracting and pulling everything else with them. Until I can't stand the pain any longer. Until the pressure of holding it in is too much. With a loud explosion, I soil myself. I let go and feel the soft, hot detritus fill my pajama trousers, spreading out in all directions, wet and clammy and full of childhood memories. Maybe that'll drive her away. Maybe the stench will be too much for her and she'll retreat. Or she'll be overcome with a wave of utter disgust for this sub-human creature before her. This befouler of his own nest.

For a moment, the plan seems to be working. Her sweet face twists and scrunches up, going from oval to eccentric. She places a handkerchief over her nose and hurries away from the bed, retreating close to the door. But it's only a tactical retreat, a temporary setback, a pause before marshalling her forces. She's only moving out of the way so that the sheet changers can charge in. Four of them this time, all practically identical, all marching in step. One pair lift me up, gingerly, one under each arm, and carry me to the nearby shower stall. There, on the cool ceramic floor, I'm stripped and hosed down, the foecal matter dissolving under the spray of sudsy water. At the same time, the other pair busy themselves with my bed: rolling the dirty sheets into a ball and replacing them with crackling duplicates that snap into place with a slingshot sound. Within a few minutes, everything is bright and clean again—and smelling of Lysol. The men troop out, hauling away the last traces of my inappropriate behavior. I follow them with infinite longing, wishing they'd haul me away, too. Wishing I, too, could be wrapped up in a ball and tossed into an industrial washing machine. The woman smiles as she sits again on my bed. As she smoothes out a wrinkle that only she sees. She smiles because she knows I've been defeated. She knows that I've done my best. Or worst. And it didn't work. She knows.

Once upon a time, she begins, in a world very much like this one—in a world exactly like this one—there lived a . . . a what?—coyote? crow? bear? blue jay? wolf? wishing well?

She looks at me, her eyes suddenly reflective pools where my fear and longing can easily be fathomed.

Help me now, she says. I know you can do it if you put your mind to it. We all can. There lived a . . . a what?

A man, I say, feeling as if the words were being ripped out of me. As if the deep tendrils were being ripped out and hauled up through my throat.

Yes! she says, clapping her hands. A man. Bravo! There lived a man. A man as in a member of the male gender of the species. And this man's name was . . . come on now . . . work with me on this . . . this man's name was . . .

Giulio, I say, my voice no louder than a mouse's squeak, no more certain than a child held under his mother's thumb.

But it doesn't matter to her. She's beaming now, grinning from ear to ear. She's happy now. She knows that, once she has me talking like any ordinary human being, my salvation can't be very far behind. At least, if she has anything to do with it.

See how easy it is, she says as she places her hand on my knee. It's warm even through the cotton pyjamas. If you put your mind to it, that is. Once you accept that you're not alone and that others can help you. That others are there for you when you need them. It's the easiest thing in the whole world, isn't it? Almost as easy as apple pie—if not quite as tasty. Hah, hah.

I'm about to smile along with her, hoping to get into her good books, when she suddenly becomes very serious—to the point of scowling.

Your story, she says, pushing her face right up against mine, almost as if trying to mimic some form of sexual intensity which she couldn't otherwise feel.

Or maybe it has nothing to do with sexual intensity. Maybe she sincerely wants to help me discover who I really am.

Tell me your story, she says, her eyes locked on mine. Please. I need to hear it. And it'll make you feel better, too. Promise.

I lean back against the wall, hoping for inspiration. Or for anything really: My name is Mary Jane and I live down the lane. What's my number? Cucumber. Come on, come on, I say to myself. Think of something. Something a little more original.

Riverrun, the scratching whispers, past Eve and Adam's . . .

Riverrun, I repeat, staring intently into the woman's dreamy, hypnotized face. Past Eve and Adam's, from swerve of shore to bend of bay . . .

And then 628 pages later, the woman asleep, my lips parched, the scratching whispers still going strong: Given! A way a lone a last a loved a long the . .

The end, I say when I realize there's no more, when I sense the scratching is about to start all over again and I don't want to be forced to give the real ending away. Not to her anyway.

 ***

Some time afterwards (I'm not really sure how long), the woman leads me outside into the bright sunlight. I presume it's the same woman, although I have no way of knowing really as I've never managed a good look at her face. Never managed to get much further than her ankles. Afraid, I guess, of what I might find up there. She leads me outside by the arm and I stumble like someone no longer used to walking.

You're cured, she says—and let's go, launching me.

I turn to thank her but the sun blinds me and, by the time I'm able to focus again, she's gone—only the click of the glazed double doors left to indicate there was anyone there in the first place. I look down at myself instead. At least, they've returned my clothes to me, I say to myself. Even if they are starched and stiff and make me feel like a zombie. And my good old bag with the name tag on it. I stand there, unsure of where to go next. From around the corner comes a man on a motorcycle. He screeches to a halt in front of me. I don't recognize him at first—what with his helmet on and all. But the moment he gets off the bike and starts walking towards me, I know exactly who it is. I drop my bag and rush into his arms.

You didn't leave me, I say. He nods. You waited all this time for me? He nods again. And takes out a sign: "Come on. Norma's waiting for you."

He hands me a spare helmet. I climb onto the back of the bike and hang on tight.

XVI. His life in two chapters

Chapter The First: The video

SCENE ONE:

[Wide-angled shot. Somewhat distorted and meant to appear menacing. Or at least mysterious and shadowy. Late afternoon from the slant of the light. Or perhaps early evening on a late summer day. Clouds billowing up over the horizon like giant fists, frothing, foaming, swirling past at breakneck speed. Trees whipping to and fro. The music, at first very loud and insistent; then fading into the background for a while before coming back strong towards the end. It starts with Beethoven's Symphony #5 in C Minor, Op. 67—Egmont Overture. Then blends into Bob Dylan's Sad-Eyed Lady Of The Lowlands. The camera swoops in from above as if mounted on wings, gliding, hovering, circling. Like a hawk perhaps or other bird of prey. A hilltop cemetery, covered with worn-away and tumbled headstones and several decayed crypts, doors hanging on single rusted hinges.]

VOICE-OVER
A man and a woman are standing there, holding hands and turning slowly as one. Or at any rate it seems that way through the camera eye—like they're at the centre of this particular universe and everything else spins around them—including the onrushing clouds. As the camera makes its descent from above, the faces become recognizable (at least for anyone who's been diligently following the story so far). One is the character called **GIULIO**; the other a woman who has remained nameless, who has been known up until now only as his **WIFE**.

[From their appearance, it doesn't look at all as if they've just emerged from one of the crypts. Or are ready to collapse into one. Both are quite young, in the prime of life. Thin, buoyant, full of energy and an unshakable belief in themselves. He's wearing brown bell-bottom trousers and a multi-colored shirt, topped by a tie of psychedelic intensity; she's in a long, red, velvet dress that accentuates nicely her breasts and hips and brings out the natural flush in her cheeks, the incipient freckles ready for sun-activation. His hair is dark and curly and rich, though already showing signs of thinning beneath the luxuriant foliage; hers another shade of red, normally straight and languid but lacquered in place for the occasion.]

VOICE-OVER

The contrast to the grey surroundings should be obvious from the moment we set eyes on them. And, though the camera might have made it seem in the beginning as if this is truly their own particular universe, the impression on closer contact is that they really don't belong here. That they've been plucked bodily from somewhere else and brought to this desolate hilltop for purposes as yet unknown. At the same time, there's the possibility they don't realize the situation they're in; that, still so enrapt in one another and the blind arrogance of young love, the world outside their circle only exists in fits and starts. And on their terms.

GIULIO
(leaning forward to kiss her)

Cucarachas!

WIFE
(returning his kiss)

Mothers-in-law!

[They push their mouths together hard and then the rest of their bodies, a grope that soon has them lying on the ground, enmeshed with one another.]

GIULIO
(unbuttoning the front of her dress to expose a blood-red half-bra)

Lactate infenestration!

WIFE
(fumbling with his belt)
Meat wagon sicophantasies!

[GIULIO runs his tongue along the top of her breast, then reaches in and pops it out of its half-cup. He takes the nipple in his mouth and begins to suck gently—at the same time slipping a hand beneath her dress. His WIFE tugs at his trousers and soon has them below his buttocks, hairy swaggerers with a life of their own. She hikes up her dress, now brown and mud-stained, and pulls him towards her.]

GIULIO
(starting to pump back and forth)
Cata-cata-cata-tonic!

WIFE
(between yelps and flesh-slapping sounds)
Cata-cata-cata-strophic!

[Their love-making becomes a blur as the camera speeds up the action to an impossible tempo. The clouds are now zooming across the screen and the sun and the moon rise and fall and rise again in a matter of moments. Then, it all slows down again, back to GIULIO and his WIFE on the ground. People begin to materialize around them. Whether popping from the air or rising from the earth is not certain as it takes place too fast for the eye to follow. First, a MIDDLE-AGED COUPLE in peasant clothing—very starched and clean but also very worn, the man holding a covered basket, the woman a squalling baby. Then, a YOUNG GIRL of no more than 10 or so, in a wedding gown and carrying a red bucket before her, as far from herself as possible. Finally, a VERY OLD MAN, dressed in ragged furs and with tiny bones in his scraggly white hair, and wielding a carved staff which also seems made of bone or ivory. While the others stand in silence watching, he circles GIULIO and his WIFE, the striking of his bare feet on the ground the only sound. After going around them once in one direction and then back in the other, he joins the three standing there.]

VERY OLD MAN
(holding the staff high over his head.
In a merry tone and full of humour)

"The Mass of Interment:
Lo, the Day of Wrath, that day,
Shall the world in ashes lay;
David thus and Sibyl say.
Oh, how great shall be the fear,
When at last, as Judge severe,
Christ the Lord shall reappear!
When the trumpet's wondrous sound,
Ringing through each burial ground,
All shall call the Throne around.
Death and Nature then shall quake
As the Dead from dust awake,
To their Judge reply to make."

[Lowers his staff over **GIULIO** and his **WIFE**. In a stentorian voice that echoes from the hilltop to the valley below.]

"This is the story of Crow:
Crow wanted to be born—he wants to make the world!
So he made himself into a pine needle.
A slave brings water to that girl, and one time he gets water with a pine needle in it.
She turns it down—makes him get fresh water.
Again he brings it. Again a pine needle is there.
Four times he brings water, and each time it's there.
Finally she just gave up—she spit that pine needle out and drank the water.
But it blew into her mouth, and she swallowed it.
Soon that girl is pregnant."

[He bursts into laughter and begins to dance about wildly. Each time he looks down at **GIULIO** and his **WIFE**, he laughs again—at one point so hard he falls down on his knees and rolls around, all the while holding his stomach. The **PEASANT WOMAN** places the bawling baby beside **GIULIO** and his **WIFE** and then vanishes, an evaporation. The baby immediately stops crying and begins to coo instead, reaching out towards the sky with his fat little fingers—as if it were actually possible to grab hold of it. The **PEASANT MAN** uncovers the basket and places it on the side opposite the baby. He too disappears in a puff of mist. In the basket are two hearts, their valves and aortas intertwined and connected together in some way. They're still beating, pumping blood through one another—to the rhythm of the couple making love. The **YOUNG GIRL** rushes up, makes as if to hurl the contents of the bucket at **GIULIO** and his **WIFE** and then is gone, flying up into the air. Nothing comes out of the bucket. Yet slowly a red, membranous cocoon, within which their shadow play can still be vaguely seen as if in a dream, forms around the two of them. The cocoon becomes thicker and more opaque until it envelopes them completely. The **VERY OLD MAN** abruptly stops rolling about and laughing. He rises, suddenly much more decrepit and hardly able to keep himself erect without the support of his staff. Bits of him are being left behind—or being eaten away.]

VERY OLD MAN
(as he begins to fall apart)
"This is a Raven story:
That Raven lay dead there for a long time, and then
Magpie, Camp Robber, and Dipper flew to him.
They just shit all over him.
They kept doing it until Raven woke up.
'What's the matter with you guys, doing that to me?
I just laid my head down.
I was sleeping there.'
'Sure, you weren't sleeping.
They killed you.
You were lying there dead.
That's why we were doing that to you,' they told him.
'What bad things are you saying!
How could I die?' he said.
Magpie and the others flew away."

(He lets out one last guffaw.)
"Pima Oriole Song 47:

And now we stop singing and scatter.
Wind springs from our singing place,
runs back and forth,
erasing the marks of people.
There's nothing left in the end."
"The Mass of Internment:
When the cursed, at Thy behest,
Go to flames that never rest,
Call me Thou to join the Blest."

[The **VERY OLD MAN** sighs and dissolves into the ground, leaving only his staff behind. The staff cracks the dry earth, splitting the headstones and the crypts and submerging them. In their place, flowers burst into bloom. Not just a few flowers—a tremendous grove of flowers, rainbow-colored, covering the entire hilltop, lifting the ever-thickening cocoon, the cooing baby, the entwined hearts. The camera pulls away. Circling skyward, to reverse the start of the scene. The clouds fly backwards, faster and faster, to their place of origin. The flowers climb higher and higher, carrying in their tentacles the captured objects. The sun and the moon rise and fall and rise and fall again. Music builds to a crescendo for 15 seconds or so. Then silence. The screen shrinks to nothing, folding in on itself.]

SCENE TWO:

[Very tight shot—practically up against their faces—of a casually-dressed group of people sitting around a coffee table. Perhaps half a dozen or so. Some are sipping on beer or mixed drinks in glasses filled with ice; others are talking and laughing loudly. Too loudly. The music at the moment is a very scratchy version of Janis Joplin's "Try (Just A Little Bit Harder)". Among the group is **GIULIO**. Older now, in his early thirties perhaps—like the others in the room. Hair still curly and black but considerably thinner. Face gaunt and eyes lacklustre. Sagging. He seems distracted, staring off, holding a beer bottle lightly by the neck, barely listening to the stories and jokes being told. When someone speaks to him, he grins half-heartedly and slumps back, gazing at the ceiling. Camera pulls back to reveal a very sparse room in a sparse house. The walls are made of bare concrete blocks, the floor a slab of painted cement, broken only by a ragged carpet depicting a scene from a safari: giant lion rearing back on its hind legs and the great white hunter about to put it out of its misery. It's dusk. Through the slatted windows can be seen thatched huts, the shadows of bonfires and naked, glistening dancers.]

VOICE-OVER

The contrast between the brown, mud-caked bodies outside and the casual white ones around the coffee table should be accentuated to the fullest: there is no meeting point, no place where they can intersect.

[Joplin is now belting out "Get It While You Can". One of the women is singing along, "letting loose" and doing the singer's famous onstage contortions. She falls forward on her knees, hair whipping the face of the man who sits across from her. A magic moment. The others clap and cheer her on. She grips his thighs and makes it seem as if she's singing directly at his crotch. Several bare-bellied children have pushed their faces right up against the glass front door of the house, desperate to understand the ritual. GIULIO gets up and heads for the front door. The children scatter. He looks out. In the distance, the sun is gleaming on a river, casting its last rays like nets. Men standing on the prows of rickety boats float by. A woman wrapped in a colorful blanket walks towards the water, a large clay bowl balanced perfectly on her head. She stoops down and lowers the bowl into the water. Then, in one motion and without even the slightest splash, lifts it back onto her head. The sun now gleams off her head, off the miniature ocean atop her head. In the area in front of the huts, men are leaping up and down to the beat of a single drum. Fiercely, as if their lives depend on it. Or perhaps their very souls. Behind them, the women squat and pound pieces of yam for the next day's meal. Without missing a beat, one of the WOMEN looks up. Her eyes glow in the dusk, glittering as if speckled with golden particles.]

VOICE-OVER

Giulio knows she's staring directly at him. He has no doubt of it. [They make eye contact.]

Giulio sees himself reflected in her eyes. But not as a physical human being. Rather as a bundle of contradictory emotions, as some form of raw energy whirling about and searching for a home. He feels himself flowing towards her along the line of sight, feels himself melting. Then she lowers her head again and it's over. Contact is broken.

[GIULIO turns back towards the people in the room. They're into a game of charades now, with one of them standing in the middle and making frantic gestures with his fingers. The diesel-fuel generator kicks in with a loud cough; the lights flicker and come to life. Or half-life really as they never actually attain full wattage. A frightened lizard scurries further up the wall, away from a cat that's determined to make a meal of it, a cat that's leaping for all it is worth—again and again. The MAN in the middle makes a scolding gesture with his finger. Then points to the corner of the room.]

JANIS JOPLIN WOMAN
(crying out and clapping her hands)

Teacher!

[Everyone cheers and she bows deeply, her breasts jiggling beneath the loose blouse. GIULIO takes a gulp of his beer and walks across the room, going from light to shadow. He walks down a corridor that separates this room from the others. Now, it's really dark and he can hardly see in front of him. He makes it to the bathroom, however, where a dim light glows from a candle on the rim of the water tank. He sits on the toilet bowl with its constant drip and its ring of eternal rust. He sits and stares: the roughly-finished and un-painted walls; the cracks where the wasps have made their nests; the long, black line of ants that uses the house as part of its territory. Out of the corner of his eye, he sees something coming out of the bath drain. A snake? They often find their way up the dry pipes. But, no. It's something antennate and ancient, very, very ancient. A shiny COCKROACH, huge for its kind—perhaps four inches long. Cautiously, it crawls out, golden wings held tight against its segmented body. It sniffs the air with its sensory feelers, making sure nothing's moving, nothing that can do it damage. Then, it begins to slide and slither across the rotting porcelain of the bath tub, unable to get a really good grip with its multiple legs. It comes up against the edge of the tub and stops for a moment, frozen, waving its cerci.]

GIULIO

Hello, Gregor. Feel like talking?

[Instead of instantly fleeing, the **COCKROACH** rises up on its last two pairs of legs, rises up until it starts to grow. Until it seems as large as **GIULIO** himself. Or at least on the same level as him. Then its insect face begins to contort, to twist and morph until it resembles a human face, albeit a very old, very wrinkled, very ugly human face.]

COCKROACH
(wearily, as if hardly able to hold this size and position
for more than a few moments at a time)
Three hundred twenty million years. Through thick and thin. We even had our own "age", you know. The "age of the cockroach". And we managed to survive that, too. That's the only antidote for angst. So don't talk to me about fathers who are unforgiving. Or mothers who abandon their offspring at birth. Let the little nymphs squirm if they're able—and die if they're not!

[The **COCKROACH** slithers down and back, once again nothing more than a four-inch giant of his kind. Head first, it scuttles into the drain and vanishes. **GIULIO** rubs his eyes. Too late, he rushes to the drain and rams a thin stick down its throat. He jams the stick up and down. Then stops to inspect it closely, to see if there are any green guts sticking to it.]

GIULIO

Bastard! And here I thought you were a friend of mine.

[**GIULIO** pours water down the toilet so that he can flush it. At the last moment, he places the empty bucket on top of the bath-tub drain. Then he walks back out along the corridor that divides the living room from the bedrooms. He can hear the people in the living room. They're getting louder and louder as the beer and hard alcohol start to have their effect. The laughter is high and almost out of control; the words garbled and slurred. Outside, the fires are still burning and the drummers are still drumming and the dancers are still dancing. From where he's standing, **GIULIO** sees them all as shadows: the inside people and the outside people. They have little substance: dark, burnt images reflected against chalky walls, gaunt and Hiroshima-like.]

GIULIO
(to no one in particular—to the lizard on the ceiling perhaps or the bats chattering overhead)
And what explosions have torn you apart, my friends? What unaspirated aspirations have compelled you to come all the way out here to be burnt shadows on a wall?

[**GIULIO** doesn't wait for an answer. He continues to walk towards back of the house and the bedrooms. The shadows vanish, the dark is all encompassing here. All that can be seen by the light of a jaundiced moon is his face, close to the wall which he uses to guide himself, hand over hand.]

VOICE-OVER
Like some blind mime after the performance is over. Like some blind mime who perhaps doesn't know the performance is over.

[Soon, the laughter and loud talking behind him sound as if they're coming from another world. A cool breeze rises, stirring the diaphanous drapes, and makes it way through the corridor. He shivers, hugging himself, but continues nevertheless. He comes to the first bedroom. The door is open—there is, in fact, no door, just a wide, yawning space between the roughly plastered walls. He looks in. A young child is sleeping, curled on the bed beneath the mosquito netting. A blonde-haired young child of three or four perhaps, breathing delicately through her nose. He steps back, then moves on to the next bedroom. It is also open. Now, by the light of the same moon, he can barely make out two figures sitting on the edge of the bed. They are sitting on the edge of the bed and they are kissing one another. Gently, but with obvious passion. The man is facing him; the woman has her back to him. Her hand is on the nape of the man's neck, lightly, tenderly, almost as if she's so much in love she's afraid to hurt him. Despite the fact her back's to him, it's easy to see the woman is **GIULIO's WIFE**. Close-up of **GIULIO's** face. He wants to cry out. Vision of him crying out like a desperate man, falling to his knees and lifting his arms into the air as he screams out of pain and pity. He wants to make the world tumble about him. Vision of him as a giant walking through the city, knocking the buildings down with a sweep of his hand. He wants to wreak havoc like some angry Olympian betrayed by one of those fragile creations he constantly trips over. Vision of him holding his **WIFE** between his thumb and forefinger. He wants to do all this. Instead, he shuts his eyes and leans back against the nearest wall. Vision of himself also on that bed—with the two of them. Under the sheets now, making love to his **WIFE** who doesn't really notice because she is making love to the **OTHER MAN** beneath a light that is grey and dusty and futureless. And the camera pulls back from them, back to him leaning against the wall, his hand slowly unzipping his trousers, slowing reaching in, slowly pulling out his engorged penis. Close-up of his face: a combination of ecstasy and hate, a glazing over of the eyes like an animal in the midst of rutting. Crickets. Sounds of laughter, clapping, dancing, drumming. Fade to darkness. Sounds shut down one at a time: first drumming, then dancing, then clapping, then laughter. Finally, only the crickets. A screech like death cry. A shudder like the giving up of some ghost. And silence.]

Chapter The Second: The Game

VOICE-OVER

Instructions: The game is very easy to play. You decide what happens next to our hero GIULIO. Just follow along before you on the screen while he goes through the ritual of daily life. Every once in a while you'll come to a junction. Or rather GIULIO comes to a junction. A place of forking. When that happens, he freezes and is unable to move. It's up to you to get him going again, to choose what you want him to do next. You have ten seconds to do so. The options are clearly laid out for you. Just click on one and away he goes on his merry way. If you don't like any of the options provided, feel free to come up with your own. Hopefully, by then, you should have as much knowledge of any particular situation as it is possible to give through the drop-down text, thus reducing the unexpected. Of course, that doesn't mean there won't be unforeseen circumstances resulting from your decisions. In fact, this is a game of unforeseen circumstances. Ready? Okay, press the green button and let's begin.

[**Level One (Park Extension):**

GIULIO is walking along the street, hands in pocket and head in the air, happy-go-lucky and carefree. He's so happy he's actually whistling. And why shouldn't he be? He's a young man with the whole future laid ahead of him—at least that's what the drop-down text says about him: "Giulio, a 21-year-old male. Bright, well-educated, healthy, in the prime of life. Ready to take the world by the tail and spin it out into space. Ready to make a difference. To leave something lasting behind." Who could ask for more? He's also happy because he's walking over to his girlfriend's house and his girlfriend's mother won't be there and there's a good chance they'll be able to have sex—in a real bed rather than under a cold park bench or on a smelly old mattress in the basement. He turns onto an overpass, the final hurdle before he arrives at the street where his girlfriend lives. It's a train overpass. The drop-down text says: "Train overpasses are a very important element in Park Ex life as they create the district's distinct boundaries on two sides, two sides that meet at slightly less than a 90 degree angle." At the top of the overpass, at its highest point, **GIULIO** stops for a moment to look down. He can see two sets of tracks running parallel (or as close to parallel as possible) to each other as far as the eye can follow. If he squints and then opens his eyes quickly, he can make the tracks snake about like black licorice sticks. **GIULIO** continues on his way, the hardest part of his journey over—all downhill from here on in. Suddenly, out of the sky, there descends a vicious-looking Samurai warrior, covered in spike-like armor and wearing a lizard-head helmet. The warrior stands solidly blocking **GIULIO**'s way, legs apart, sword weaving menacingly in the air. Slowly, it removes its helmet. Surprise! The Samurai warrior turns out to be his **GIRLFRIEND**. Before **GIULIO** can ask what this is all about, what's the big idea, she smiles and turns sideways, sword tip planted in the ground. Her profile shows a definite swelling around the area of her belly, a swelling that seems to be growing bigger by the moment. The drop-down text says: "Reproduction: a process whereby living plant or animal cells or organisms produce offspring. Reproduction is one of the essential functions of living organisms, as necessary for the preservation of the species as food getting is for the preservation of the individual."

GIULIO:
A. Turns and flees in horror, pulling out his hair in clumps and shrieking.
B. Laughs bitterly in her face and then eviscerates himself on her sword.
C. Pulls out his own sword and engages her in hand-to-hand combat.
D. Leaps over her and continues walking, as happy and carefree as ever (though now uncertain of his final destination).
E. Tries to explain in a reasonable and sensible way why he can't commit himself and is viciously attacked for his troubles.
F. Manages to convince her to have "a termination" before the inevitable emotional attachment kicks in.
G. Manages to convince her to give the child up for adoption—preferably in some far-off place like China.
H. Squats down before her and goes into a deep Zen hibernation which no Samurai shouts, grunts or threats can penetrate.
I. Opens the nearest manhole cover and descends into it, slinking off into the lower depths.
J: None of the above.

(Sufficient blank space reserved here so you can fill in for yourself what you think is **GIULIO**'s best course of action under the circumstances. Remember: he can't fly or suddenly develop the power of omniscience or immortality. But he can go off on a tangent, shift gears, change direction, head for the hills)].

You move from one option to the other. What to do? Come on, now. It's not that difficult, is it? Just choose one. Doesn't matter if it's not the best one. Just—The screen explodes into thousands of little bits, sending the images flying in all directions like pieces from a mirror. Then it goes blank. A message flashes: "Too late. If you wish to try again, press the green button."

• • • • •

[Level XXX (The Farm):

Middle-aged **GIULIO** is digging his way through the snow. He is digging from the house towards the barn—some fifty metres away. There's a light in the barn, glowing brightly despite the storm. A lantern, maybe, fuelled by trusty kerosene. Behind him, standing in the kitchen window, is his **WIFE**, barefoot and wrapped in a fluffy wool bath robe. She's smiling and waving at him. But he doesn't notice, so pre-occupied is he with removing the snow. With clearing a path to the barn where the chickens wait to be fed. The drop-down menu says: "Giulio knows he should buy a snowblower of some kind, even if only a small electric one. But something tells him he mustn't. That the introduction of a new device would endanger the whole wonderful structure he's managed to build up through the years. Nothing can dissuade him. The feeling is overpowering, as if ingrained in him from birth. Or at least from the time he has conscious memories." He finally makes it to the barn and, for a moment, just stands there, leaning on the shovel and enjoying the shelter from the wind. The sweat begins to dry on him, giving him the chills. He'd like to light a cigarette perhaps, to suck in the satisfying aroma of nicotine and the potpourri of other chemical poisons. But he doesn't smoke so that particular pleasure is denied him. Instead, he takes in a deep breath, feels the cold air burning his lungs. Then he enters the chicken coop. The rooster, a cock-eyed S.O.B. whose coxcomb tilts always to one side, makes an aggressive move towards him. But then thinks better of it, remembering that swift kick from the previous time he'd tried it. In the dim light, seething with dust motes, **GIULIO** turns to scoop up a handful of corn from the metal barrel. It is then that he spots, curled in the far corner:

A. A dead rat, stiff and extended, tail like a pointed rod, buck-teeth in their last half-gnaw.
B. A pixie, its light still glowing faintly, an aura of confusion and diminished magical powers in a world that no longer wants it.

C. The body of his mother, crippled hands folded across her chest and a heavenly smile on her face.

D. The sacrificed God in all his/her/their glory, still nailed to the rough plank.

E. Quetzalcoatl's molted skin and a few bloodied feathers.

F. His mother's body, twisted and contorted in the anguish of not having got her own way in the end.

G. The raven and the coyote, mounted on a varnished piece of wood, snarling at each other in bitter and unrelenting hatred, all beak and talon and fang and claw.

H. A man in a wheelchair, spinning uselessly, arms reaching out as if asking for help. Or perhaps offering help—it's always hard to tell these things.

I. Other: fill in as you see appropriate. Only no angels please. We've had a glut of them lately.]

Once again, you feel helpless. This game just isn't for you. You hate making decisions. Why can't all the options be true? Why can't—This time the screen doesn't just go blank, it begins to shout at you: "Idiot! Moron! Nincompoop! Lucky you're not in the cockpit of a jet fighter. You'd have been dead a long time ago." It repeats this message several times.

• • • • •

[Level Pen-Ultimate (The Forest):

An old, wizened **GIULIO** is struggling to jog beneath the sun-dappled canopy of an immense evergreen forest. The sound of his heavy breathing can be heard above the rustle of pine cones and the indignant swaying of spruce trees as the wind soughs through them. Somewhere in the distance a river rushes. Headlong. The drop-down menu says: "No longer so happy-go-lucky but still feeling fortunate, Giulio trots along a narrow path that has been cut out of the heavy underbrush and marked with purple ribbons. If he really wanted to, he could deviate from this path because the forest is clear under the protective branches. And the ground is covered with pine needles. But it wouldn't be easy, especially at his age. And there's no telling when the non-path would become impenetrable. Or would lead to the sharp, deep edge of an inland lake, all cliff and plummeting silences. Or would put him in direct conflict with a stray wolf or an irritated bear looking for a good hibernation spot. So, for the time being, **GIULIO** is happy sticking to the path." He goes up and down the hilly terrain, passing at one point quite close to a small brook. After about half an hour, he comes out into a natural clearing. The clearing is two hundred metres wide or so, a field choked with flowers. **GIULIO** fancies himself somewhat of an expert and quickly spots white wake-robin and nodding trilliums, maidenhair ferns, musk thistles, Canada goldenrods, raspberry bushes and a stand of northern fox grapes, wrapped around a dead tree. He stops for a moment to pick the grapes. They're juicy but very sour, making his mouth pucker. As he starts up again, he spots someone at the far end of the clearing just vanishing back into the forest. **GIULIO** tries to pick up his pace—but he can't really go much faster. The drop-down menu says: "The appearance of someone else in the forest startles Giulio because never before, in all his years of jogging, has he encountered anyone on this trail. He rubs his eyes, thinking they might be deceiving him—an old man's rheumy old eyes, fit only for watering. But no. He once again spots the man's back before him. Now, he's determined to catch him, to jog along with him for a while, to engage him in conversation, to perhaps make plans to meet again the next day." **GIULIO** puts on a spectacular burst. Or he thinks it's a spectacular burst. And yes, he does make some progress. "Hey," he shouts hoarsely. "Wait up." The man doesn't hear him, just continues on his steady way, arms pumping almost mechanically, legs rhythmically moving forward. **GIULIO** has to admire the way the man jogs. A veteran, someone who could probably teach him a few tricks. He comes to the final rise. It's downhill from this spot on. **GIULIO** doesn't so much pick up his speed as stumble forward, afraid to stop for fear he'll lose whatever balance he has left and land on his head. It doesn't matter. All that counts is that he's gaining. Steadily. He can see the man very clearly now ahead of him, ducking and weaving among the low-lying branches. He's only fifty metres away now. Only forty. Only thirty. The man's broad back fills the path before him. Only twenty. **GIULIO** wants to call out again but he can't. All his energy is concentrated in his legs, his thighs, his chest. If he loses that concentration, it's over. He knows that. He'll simply stagger over to one side and be unable to resume his pace. Only ten.

GIULIO reaches out with one arm, still stumbling forward. Almost close enough to touch him now. Almost close enough . . . Without slowing down, the man turns to face GIULIO. He turns and holds out his hand—like a runner about to accept or pass the baton. GIULIO pulls up. It is:

A. A friend of GIULIO's, with whom he has cinnamon cappuccino every afternoon at precisely three o'clock.
B. A complete stranger, who smiles gently and then steps out of the way, so that GIULIO can continue to stumble along.
C. A recently-paroled repeat child molester, whose likeness GIULIO has on his jogging suit, marked with a large 'X'.
D. GIULIO himself, at a younger stage in his life. Say, the middle-aged GIULIO, glimpsing out of the corner of his eye the peek-a-boo rays of mortality. Or the GIULIO just about to get married, shaking the snow from his suit. Or the young man GIULIO on a train heading West. Or even the young child GIULIO, floating on his raft towards the headwaters of a deadly river.
E. A man with no face. A vague, light brown oval where his face should be. A blank where his face should be. A light brown blank where his face should be. An emptiness as disturbing as any gnarled monster. Beetle grub. Snake skin. Bird with a maggot hooked to its beak.
F. Sorry, that's it. The lot. No other option available].

This time you're ready for it. You click on A and wait. Nothing happens. Immediately, you click on B. Yes, that must be right. The right option. Complete strangers are usually harmless. Still nothing. You click on C, shuddering at the thought of having to face this repeat offender and grateful not to have any children of your own. And nothing as yet. D, then. D, in desperation—though you don't know what it means for the hero to see himself at a younger stage in his life. For a moment, you think you see the image of a naked man sitting on a chair—but then it's gone again. You click on E. Why not? Maybe you can be the one to finally give this poor creature a human face. Nothing at all. Everything still frozen: This old man about to touch the other and the other half-turned towards him. Finally, F. It must be F. The message says: "No other option available here. Simply click on any of the above for the screen to go dark. Or just wait a few moments and it'll go dark on its own. Without you having to do a thing."

No! you scream. That's not what I want. That's not the way I want it to end. Take me back to that clearing. Please, I want to see that clearing again. I need to write down the names of those wild flowers. That's it. Otherwise, I'll never remember them. It will have been a lesson completely lost on me.

You bang around the buttons. Punch at them as hard as you can. Try different combinations. Green, red, blue. Petulantly kick at the metal housing for the screen. But it does no good. None of it does any good. After a few moments, the screen flashes: "Game over. Game over. Game over. The Ultimate Level just isn't for you, I'm afraid. But, you did manage to win some extra lives through your persistence and determination (well, actually, everybody does). So maybe you'll get another chance one of these days. Won't that be nice? Won't that be nice? Won't that be nice?"

XVII. Homeward bound

I'm curled up in a thin, tattered sleeping bag, shivering against the damp and cold. Even my head's buried and zippered shut. There's the patter of rain beating on the bag, sometimes heavy, sometimes light. Already, it's hard to find spots that aren't soaked. But that's okay. It could be worse. It could be ice and snow like a couple of weeks ago. The ground's hard and lumpy beneath me. Sharp objects are pushing against my back and side, jabbing me no matter which way I turn. All around me, I can hear the sounds of traffic and the splashing of water. Reluctantly, without enthusiasm, I unzipper the bag and peek my head through the opening. Just as I thought: cars and rain. I slowly ease myself out until I'm halfway sitting up and leaning against the side of a building. Nothing's changed from yesterday or the day before or the day before that. The people still circle around me, rushing this way and that. The news vendor still sits in her little shed, listening to the audio portion of "Coronation Street" on the radio. The hot dog and sausage seller still paces back and forth, like a juggler trying to keep all his plates a-twirling. And that woman still marches up and down in front of the building, carrying a sandwich sign that says: "You took my children away just because I was poor. Give them back." A man with an umbrella stops a few feet away from her, shakes the umbrella impressively from side to side and then carries on into the building. A bunch of private school children, all dressed in blue blazers, are being herded from one historic financial site to another. Well, I presume they're historic financial sites anyway. Why else would they be teaching private school children about them? Those kids have no time to lose. Every moment is precious as they climb the pre-corporate ladder. I, on the other hand, have all the time in the world. In a couple of hours, I'll rise in a leisurely fashion and make my way to the nearest hospice. There, a hot meal will be waiting and a place to hang my sleeping bag. It never really dries properly though. But it's the thought that counts. Perhaps, today, I'll run into my black-coated, gunslinger friend. Or Norma, making her rounds. Perhaps, one of them will have a room where we can lie down for a while side by side and listen to the hiss of the gas heater. That's always a treat on days like this. But I'm not counting on it. I've learned that counting on things is a sure way for them not to come true. Best to let the world surprise you: with blows, if it must; with hugs and kisses on the rare occasion.

Oh well. I pull myself up, still making sure to keep the sleeping bag wrapped around me. A woman with a small child walks by. The child, all blonde curls and Shirley Temple dimples, reaches out and drops a few coins at my feet. I thank her with a nod—and another to the woman I presume is her mother. I'm about to make my way down the street, in the direction of the closest soup kitchen, when a bus stops right in front of me, blocking my path. One of those multi-colored charter buses with the psychedelic windows. Great, I think. Now I'm going to have to detour into the street. Have more water splashed on me by motorists who get a real kick out of doing things like that. The bus door opens with a swoosh of hydraulics. Good, now I can give the driver hell.

Is your name Giulio? he asks, all friendly like and gleaming white teeth, before I have a chance to confront him.

That's what they call me, I say, too startled to challenge him or to demand to know how he learned my name.

Express bus, he says, wiping the sweat off his brow. All aboard for Montreal.

Montreal?

Montréal, he says, pronouncing it French-style.

What are you talking about? I don't know what you're talking about. I begin to walk around the bus. Montreal? Why should I want to go to Montreal?

He looks at me and gives a big sigh—as if he's feeling sorry for me or something. Then he stares down at his big feet, one poised above the gas, the other ready for the clutch.

This is how it works, see, he says, sounding tired. If you're Giulio, then this is the express bus to Montreal. Now, either you get on it or it goes without you. He glances down at his watch, then back at me. You've got ten seconds.

He begins to count down, very calmly. Like he's done this sort of thing before. He's reached "two" and is preparing to shut the door when I finally shed my sleeping bag and jump onboard.

What the hell, I say. I ain't got nothing to lose. Besides, I've always wanted to see Montreal.

That's the spirit. Now, brace yourself. We're flying here. We've got a lot of time to catch up on.

No sooner am I onboard, however, than I remember something I've left behind. Something very important.

My bag! I shout. We've gotta stop for my bag. All my clothes and shit.

The bus driver once more gives me that look of feeling sorry for me. Then, without taking his eyes off the highway, he jerks his head towards the back of the bus. On the seat behind me is my blue bag. I recognize it by the name tag. Outside on the sidewalk, the man in the black coat, more gaunt and bird-like than ever, is waving at me. He flashes a giant card that reads: "Good luck. Don't forget your friends." Behind him, Norma is leaning against the very same building where I'd been poised only moments before. She's leaning with one leg straight and the other bent at the knee, the toe of rotted boot barely touching the ground. There are sweat and grease stains on the armpits of her jacket, the same bursting at the seams jacket she was wearing on another bus so long ago. Head down, she's holding a cigarette in one hand and a videocassette in the other. The video-cassette has been gutted, tape trailing everywhere. She looks up for a moment, then lowers her head again, at the same time dropping the videocassette onto the street. I press my face against the window as hard as I can, squashing my lips against it. My friend laughs and blows me a kiss. Norma gives me the finger. The bus pulls out.

• • • • •

It seems I barely have time to shut my eyes when the driver announces our arrival at the Montreal terminus.

Home, he says, as the door opens with a satisfied swoosh. *Vous êtes arrivez.*

Home? Warmth? Shelter? Feelings of belonging? Of kinship? I try to conjure some up. Could it have something to do with the churning in the pit of my stomach? The dryness at the back of my throat? Nah. That's just hunger and thirst.

Ah, I say all nonchalant and coy-like, if it's alright with you, I think I'll just stay on the bus. Okay?

Nope, he says. End of the line. Your ticket's not valid for the return journey. Not at this time anyway. So, be a good boy and get off my bus.

He stands up, suddenly holding a billy club in his hand. I take the hint and step down, bag gripped tightly.

That's a good boy, he says, sitting back down. I knew you weren't going to cause trouble. Good-bye—and good luck. *Bon chance, eh?*

The bus pulls out again, its psychedelic colors spinning in the sunlight like one of those hypnotic wheels we used to fool around with as children. I watch it disappear in a puff of blue diesel smoke, its tail rising. I head towards the sliding doors that lead into the terminus. The reflection in the doors causes me to do a double-take. Gone are the rags and remnants, the unlaced, tongueless shoes, the Salvation Army trousers held up with a frayed cord. Now, it's brown corduroys and shiny black Oxfords and a grey turtleneck sweater. And the bag may bear some resemblance to the one I had on the bus—only this one's brand new, not held together with duct tape and a prayer. But those are the least of the surprises. The face in the doors is young. And his hair is thick, richly-curled. And he's got on a pair of granny glasses that make him look like some kind of prof from the days when profs wore those kinds of glasses. And the strangest thing of all is that none of this freaks me out. It's as if this is the most natural thing in the world. Yeah. Old bums about to fall off the edge of the universe always re-incarnate as young, quasi-professorial types in turtleneck sweaters. It's only when I step towards the doors that I notice what's really happened. The reflection doesn't belong to me at all but to a young man standing beside me, a young man holding a thick book in his hand. The same old me is right there, as scruffy and unkempt as ever. At first, I'm relieved. And then a little disappointed.

The young man goes through the doors, whistling to himself. I follow a few steps behind. Once inside, I look around. The usual bus terminus. End of the line blues. Although I imagine there's some sociology prof somewhere who's willing to argue that not all bus terminuses are the same—and there's no need to equate terminus with terminal. I'm still contemplating these deep thoughts (deep for me, at any rate) when a tall, angular black man with a cigarette dangling from the side of his mouth walks up to me. Sidles up to me, really.

Taxi? he says, like he's afraid somebody's gonna accuse him of something if they overhear.

Taxi? I say. I look around. Are you talking to me?

You want a taxi, man?

Sure, I say. Why not?

Sure? Now, why would I say that? But it's too late. He reaches for my bag and tells me to follow him. There's a whole string of cabs outside, their drivers leaning out the windows chattering or listening intently to the radio where people are shouting in languages I don't understand. He leads me to the first in line and opens the door for me.

Where to, man? he asks once I'm in the back seat.

Oh, I say. Where to? I look around—as if something in the cab will give me the inspiration I need to answer that question. The cabbie's photo and I.D.? No, that won't do. The name tag! Of course. I lift the tag and read out the address on it.

That's Park Extension, man, he says, clicking the meter to "Start".

That's right, I say with an air of authority as I lean back. I'm going home to Park Extension. It's where I come from.

Is it now? He looks at me in the mirror. I nod. Good place, man. Good place to score.

I don't know what he's talking about so I keep quiet. For the next ten minutes or so as we go up a wide boulevard with manicured parks on both sides, I watch the meter clicking away, a nickel at a time. Then, it strikes me: he's going to want to be paid at the end. That's how taxis operate, isn't it? How am I going to pay? I search my pockets for money. Nothing. I begin to panic. He might take me to the police if I can't pay. Or he might bring me to an alley somewhere where he and a bunch of his friends will beat it out of me. And no one will give a shit when they find my battered body head first in a garbage can. One less bum on the welfare rolls. I'm on the verge of complete panic—to the point where I'm considering jumping out of the moving car. I reach into the bag and search around frantically. My hand finds something square and soft and made of leather as far as I can tell. I pull it out. A wallet! And it's full of money. Thank you, Lord. I lean back, trying to slow my breathing down. Jeez, am

I always this frightened? Always in this much of a frenzy? And why hadn't I bothered looking in the bag before? All those weeks on the street when I could've been in some warm, cozy hotel.

We're here, man, he says, pulling up in front of a modest red brick house that could use some work. He looks at the meter. Eight dollars.

No problem, I say and hand him a ten dollar bill. Keep the change.

Jeez, could've had a hot meal for several days running with two bucks. Or a front-row seat at the Bawdy House & Lap Dancing Emporium. Guess I'm the magnanimous type nowadays, eh? Hey, when you've got it, you flaunt it.

After the cab drives off, I look around for a moment, up and down the street. Nothing very unusual about it: a few stunted trees; a few scraggly flower gardens; a few browning patches of grass; a few cracks in the cement. But it makes quite a change from the ones where I'd been spending most of my time lately. As I turn to head for the address on the name tag, I notice a little boy throwing sticks against the curb and then watching carefully where they fall. He can't be more than ten.

Hello, I say, shading him from the sun. What are those?

Bones, he says, not looking up at me.

Bones? They look like sticks to me.

Shows what you know, he says. He holds them in his fist. These are chicken bones. I can read your future with them. Of course, I prefer haruspication. But animal entrails are a little harder to get these days.

Go on, I say. Pull the other one.

Instead of answering, he tosses the sticks/bones against the curb. They bounce back, landing every which way. Slowly, he begins to pick them up one at a time.

Well, I say. What do you predict for me, Mr. Seer? Mr. User of Big Words? Mr. Wise Beyond His Years?

What's the world coming to, he says, standing up, when the puppet thinks he can manipulate his own strings?

What? I say, seeing myself suddenly tangled up in ropes. I didn't quite hear you. What's that about a puppet?

Nothing, he says, walking away. It was just a joke.

Oh really. Just a joke, eh?

I reach over and grab him by the collar. He's so light I can lift him without any effort. Lift him so that his legs dangle several feet above the ground.

Who sent you, you little twerp? I shake him. Huh? Come on. Before I throw <u>your</u> bones against the nearest wall—and then we'll see what sort of future <u>you've</u> got.

He stares at me as if he couldn't care less. As if the only things that interest him are those damn bones in his hands. I put him down again. He walks away as nonchalant as you please. He even stops to toss those bones one more time. I turn and climb the front steps of the red brick house. They creak beneath me, indicating incipient rot perhaps. I'm about to ring the bell when I notice the door is already open. Ajar. When is a door not a door? The old schoolboy joke still makes me giggle. I push the door and enter. The house is dark and cool. Almost mouldy. And not at all that inviting. Everything seems faded and worn: from the door frames to the chandeliers; from the wallpaper to the wood floors. I stand at the entrance, facing a short hallway. From there, I can see a yellow kitchen table, metal not wood. On the table is an empty plate and a napkin with a fork and spoon on it.

Hello, I call out. Anybody home?

A middle-aged woman peeks from the far end of the hallway. She's wearing a wrinkled kerchief and an apron speckled with red stains.

Oh, it's you, she says, wiping her hands on the apron. Just in time for supper.

In time for supper?

She ducks back in. I walk through the hallway and into the kitchen. The woman is standing before a gas stove, stirring a large pot with a wooden spoon.

Sit, she says. Your father's already eaten. You know how he can't wait. Has to make sure not to miss his blessed radio program.

She looks up as if seeking help from above. I sit down before the empty plate—I have no choice as it's the only place with a chair. The woman turns towards me, carrying a small bowl filled with sausages and meatballs. She places it on the table. Then she picks up my plate and brings it back to the stove.

Have you made up your mind yet? she asks, her back to me.

About what? I say.

You know about what.

Without bothering with oven mitts, she lifts the boiling pot from the stove and carries it to the sink. There, she runs cold water on it before tipping the contents into a colander. The pasta slides out, splashing over the sides.

Why do you run cold water on it first? I ask, genuinely curious. Doesn't that make the spaghetti cold?

It brings the starch to the top, she says as she drains the pasta and places it in my plate. She adds sauce and cheese to it and puts it in front of me.

Smells delicious, I say, digging in.

Your father doesn't know anything about it. Always the last one to know.

I don't know anything about it either, I want to say. Instead, I shrug and concentrate on winding the spaghetti strands round and round my fork.

After you're finished, maybe you should go down and tell him, she says. She wipes her hands on the apron. It might sound better coming from you.

Okay, I say.

I hope you're making the right choice, she says. You don't want to be regretting it the rest of your life.

I won't.

She pulls up a chair and sits down opposite me. There are several times when it seems she wants to say something. Or perhaps to burst into tears. It's hard to tell. But she does neither. She simply brushes strands of grey hair from her eyes and watches me eat. When I finish, she reaches over and takes the plate away.

He's in the basement, she says as she scrapes the remains into the garbage disposal. If you get him now, he won't be too far gone.

Right about now I feel like yelling at her: who the fuck are you and what the fuck are you talking about? What am I supposed to be telling this man you've described as my father? What exactly does he want to hear from me? But somehow I realize that would be taken the wrong way. As some sort of ultimate, unforgivable insult. A slap in the face to end all slaps in the face. So I decide to play along instead.

Okay, I say, pushing my chair away. I think I'll go talk to him now.

The basement stairs are rickety and not easy to negotiate in the dim light—which comes from one solitary bulb somewhere in the depths. The basement itself barely deserves the name. The floor is dirt on one side and unfinished cement on the other. The walls are damp to the touch. Greasy almost, causing me to rub my hands against my pants. Hanging from the low ceiling on sawed-off hockey sticks are braids of onions and garlic. Seeds are drying on make-shift shelves: melon, cucumber, squash, some I don't recognize. I squint. There's something familiar about the gutted mattress leaning against the far wall. Something I can't quite place. The wall itself is cracked in half, from top to bottom. Attempts have been made at sealing the crack but they haven't worked very well. Have, in fact, made it look worse—like some sort of massive scar. As I move forward, I see a second room built within the basement, a room with its own door. A light shines from beneath the door: yellow and sickly. I push it open—and am almost overpowered by the odor of fermentation, the new wine bubbling in open demi-johns or dripping from the press. A middle-aged man sits at a small wooden table on which have been placed a half-filled bottle and two glasses. He's very thin, almost hollow-cheeked and so bony I'm afraid his skin will crack open at any time. His deep-set eyes focus straight ahead, unblinking. They could be death rays they're so intense and unforgiving. He's listening to music that comes from an ornate radio, a gleaming hand-polished radio stuffed with vacuum tubes. I recognize the music as an opera—but I have no idea which one. I sit opposite him, the chair scraping the floor.

Leoncavallo, Ruggiero, he says, as if being roused from a deep sleep. *I Pagliacci.*

He pours some wine into the two glasses. Then he holds one up to the light before bringing it to his lips.

My children are afraid of me, he says, still not looking at me. And I don't blame them. All they see is a man filled with rage and bitterness and the disgust of failure. It's as if I've swallowed a package of razor blades and now I'm spitting them back out one at a time. Everything I say cuts someone to ribbons. I live in a topsy-turvy world. In a world that makes no sense. I work when others sleep; I sleep when others work. And I have no idea what to do anymore to make things right.

He looks at me at last. I don't know what he's talking about. So I don't say anything. Instead, I down my glass of wine and stand up.

My children are afraid of me, he begins again, twirling the glass on the table. And I don't blame them. All they see—

As I walk out, he continues to talk, to repeat his words of self-loathing. Then stops suddenly the moment I'm out of his line of sight.

Mascagni, Pietro, he says as the music changes abruptly. *La Cavalleria Rusticana.*

I climb the basement stairs hurriedly, almost afraid a hand is going to reach out and drag me back down. Pull me into the dark corner where the furnace lies sleeping, ready to be fed with the bodies of children who betray their parents. The feeling intensifies as I make it back to the kitchen. My breath is sharp and shallow. I have trouble getting enough air. There's something suffocating me in here. I must get out of the house. I walk past the woman in the kitchen and into the hallway. She has her head down on the table and doesn't notice me slipping by. I hurry out and lean against the brick wall, catching my breath. It's as warm as ever, the sun now directly overhead. I look up and down the street. Empty. Ghostly. Silent. At least, it seems that way for a moment. But when I blink and look again, there are suddenly people everywhere. Some are cutting their little squares of lawn, hardly able to manoeuvre the oversized mowers. Others are rocking on dilapidated balconies, creaking back and forth and back and forth. Still others are engrossed in serious renovation, hammering away at doors and windows and whatever else needs fixing. The boy with the bones is also there, sitting in the same spot as when I first met him. He signals for me to follow him. I hesitate but he insists, finally taking me by the hand and pulling me along.

Okay, okay, I say. Don't get pushy.

At the end of the street, we come to a scruffy, undersized park that faces the railroad tracks. There's the semblance of a baseball diamond but it's mostly overgrown with weeds, leaving only the base paths exposed. And the backstop is rusted and tilting dangerously. Two dogs are chasing one another in the field, taking turns sniffing and growling. The boy walks out towards them, quickly losing himself in the tall grass. On the far side of the diamond is a bench for spectators—also about to fall apart. A young man sits on it, staring out. It's only when I approach that I notice the wheelchair beside him.

Hey, he says. You made it back. Long time no see. Give me a hand here.

He struggles to shift position on the bench, inching towards the wheelchair. I hold the wheelchair steady as he plops himself into it.

There, that's better, he says, adjusting the blanket over his legs. Okay, let's go.

Where to?

Where to? he says laughing. You were always a great joker, weren't you? Remember the time with the butterflies?

Oh yeah, I say, completely at a loss, the time with the butterflies. Sure. How could I ever forget that?

I push him along, trying to picture "the time with the butterflies". Nothing comes to mind. It's only after we've gone ahead for a few minutes that I notice something strange. I could swear we'd been heading away from the red brick house. Or at least at a ninety degree angle from it. Yet here we are approaching it again.

No! I say, steering the wheelchair in the other direction.

Hey, he says, twisting to look back at me, are you alright?

Fine, I say. Just fine.

I push the chair—a little more quickly now—only to turn the corner and come once again face to face with the house. My hands fall away. I just stand there, unable to move. The man in the wheelchair looks up at me.

Remember once, he says, when you told me you'd like nothing better than to just sit and wait for things to catch up to you?

I shake my head. I don't remember saying anything of the sort. And it's not the sort of thing I'd say anyway.

Well, he says, ignoring my head shake. Here you are. Your wish has come true.

I don't know what you're talking about, I say. You've obviously mistaken me for someone else. Now, if you'll excuse me--

I walk away down the street as fast as I can—almost running. The house looms ahead of me. I turn back. It's there, at the other end, as if rising on its haunches.

You'd better go back in, the man in the wheelchair says, covering his eyes from the sun. They're waiting for you.

Who are you? I ask. Where do you know me from?

That's an old game, he says. We used to play it as kids. The street-corner in winter, remember? The greasy spoon? But it's grown pretty thin by now. Time you got yourself a new one, don't you think?

He turns the wheelchair and pushes himself away down the street.

No, I'm serious, I shout. Who do you think I am?

I don't have to think, he says. I know. And so do you, Giulio.

Giulio! I say, still shouting. Everybody calls me that. Everybody thinks I'm Giulio. But who the hell is Giulio?

He continues down the street. I want to follow. To chase him down. To spill him out of the wheelchair. To pin him to the ground and place my knee across his chest and demand some answers. But I realize immediately how useless that would be. Instead, I resign myself to walking back up the steps of the house.

Oh, it's you, the middle-aged woman says, wiping her hands on the apron as she peers out the hallway. Just in time for supper.

The plate is waiting on the table; the steam is coming from the boiling pot; the scene is ready to start all over again. But, instead of going down the hallway into the kitchen, I turn up the stairs leading to the second floor. Up the dark, bannistered stairway with the oak-leaf railing. Perhaps there's a way to escape from there. Through the roof maybe, through one of those escape hatches. I find myself on a landing onto which three doors lead—one on either side of me and one directly in front. But no escape hatches in sight. Not a single one. I open the door to my immediate left. It's a bathroom, an old-fashioned bathroom with an old-fashioned bath-tub, the type with the claws for feet. In fact, the bathroom itself doesn't really look like a bathroom. No tiles on the walls or floor. No lights over the slightly-tilted mirror. More like a room recently converted for the purpose. There's water in the tub—lots of water and about to overflow, actually. I reach down and shut off the tap. To one side is a wire contraption holding soap and shampoo. The water's very warm and very inviting. Almost hypnotic and lulling in its effect. Why not? I say to myself. What's the harm? I remove my clothes and lower myself into the tub. I just lie there for a few moments, only my nose and eyes above water. A discolored toothbrush floats by. How'd that get there? I fish it out and drop it by the side of the tub. Then I start to scrub myself: my chest, my legs, my arms, my torso. I get down on my knees and pull back my foreskin, cleaning out beneath it. The last thing is my hair. I can feel the grease and dirt as I pour the shampoo over it and suds it up. I count to three and, holding my breath, dunk my head beneath the water. I have to do this several times before all the soap is gone and my hair feels clean. Then I pull the plug and step out. Shivering in the suddenly cool air, I dry myself off quickly with a worn and paper-thin towel, still damp from previous use. I'm just about to put my clothes back on when I notice another set on a wooden chair behind the door. Odd that I didn't see them before. But it doesn't matter. These are folded and clean. That's all that counts. And they fit me nicely. A little snugly perhaps—especially the corduroy pants—but not uncomfortable. I've just slipped on the black turtle-neck sweater when I hear someone calling out my name. Or, at least the name that I seem to have inherited.

Giulio, what are you doing? Aren't you finished yet?

It's the voice of a young woman. Throaty, I think they call it. Just the sound of it causes my penis to rise and begin to harden.

Giulio, she calls out again. Hurry.

I follow the sound of her voice. It comes from the room that opens up in the middle of the landing. I turn the door knob and enter. It's a young woman alright and she's lying in bed, a white sheet pulled up to her neck.

Come on, she says, throwing the sheet aside to invite me in.

For a moment, I stand frozen. Unsure of what to do. The sight of her makes me think I've been transported to some other place. To some place where people actually make love and enjoy the touch of one another's bodies and the intimate probings and all the rest of the stuff that I can't imagine ever happening to me.

I sit down on the bed and begin to remove my clothes. My borrowed clothes. As I pull the turtle-neck off, she passes her fingers along the ridge of my spine. She starts at my nape and then slowly works her way down to my coccyx. I shiver and turn towards her, so rigid it aches. I press myself against her. She's like a furnace.

Always remember this moment, she says in my ear, her breath just brushing the lobe. Always remember the first time.

But my mind is too blank and the rest of me too pre-occupied. Suddenly, I don't care who I am or what they want me to be. I don't care if God is watching or if there's nothing out there but a dumb emptiness that goes on forever. I don't care if we have the rest of our lives to act out this moment or if someone's going to burst in at any moment. Ready to hurl a bucket of cold water on us—as if we were little more than a pair of rutting dogs. I just don't care. She pulls me on top of her, on the source of the heat. I kiss her lips, her neck, her nipples. I lick her nipples, feeling the tiny bud beneath my tongue. Then I work my way back up. She opens her legs, placing them against my sides. Her hands work away at my penis, straightening it, aiming it. I lower myself and thrust, meeting solid resistance. I persist, pushing hard. She gives a cry, a sudden burst of pain. I almost pull away. But she holds me there, holds my buttocks tight, forcing me to continue. A second thrust. The resistance gives somewhat. She grimaces. A third thrust and I'm inside her. The grimace turns into a smile. I begin to move faster and faster, my hips seemingly possessed of a mind of their own. And then there's no stopping—not even when I spot the drops of blood on the towel beneath her. Not until I've spent myself and fallen away, struggling to catch my breath.

She rises then and, holding the towel tight against her crotch, waddles a little shakily out of the room. A moment later, the flush of a toilet. Or rather, the gurgle of a toilet, indicating old piping, a leaky stop-cock, loose connections somewhere in its bowels. I lean back on the bed, thinking: This I wouldn't mind doing again and again. Not that stuff in the kitchen and basement. No sir, I could do without that. But this. I could spend the rest of my life doing this. You bet. She waddles back into the room and stands near the bed for a moment, stretching. Her legs are strong and solidly-planted, like in the paintings of old-style goddesses; her pubic hair is thick and tightly curled, with a tiny hint of red along the edges; her breasts curve up like scimitars—the left slightly more than the right—as she pulls her shoulders back; her eyes are grey-green, the irises a constellation of tiny specks floating in their separate universe; her nose has a tilt of its own, indicating fierceness and a willingness never to give up. She finishes stretching with a yawn and lowers herself onto the bed beside me: eyes shut, hands by her side, breathing gently through her nostrils, her breasts rising and falling. I want her then— like I've never wanted a woman before. Or a man, for that matter. The Normas and the black-caped friends pale before her, shrivel into scrunched-up bits of fluff. Human lint from memory's giant spin-dryer. How could I have ever desired them? I ask myself. How could I have ever lowered myself to have sex with them? She's all I want. All I'll ever want. I reach for her, prepare to once again ease myself into her. But it's not to be. My hand cuts right through her. I begin to panic. How is this possible? I find it hard to believe that just a few moments ago (or so it seems) I was penetrating her all-too-real flesh, making suck-a-sucking noises between her legs with my all-too-fleshy protuberance. Now, one of us is no longer real. And, for all practical purposes, it doesn't matter who. I lash out, punching through her and into the pillow. Again and again. I want to hurt her badly, thinking that might bring her back to me, that might allow us to touch again. And so I tire myself out punching away at the pillow, burying my fist into it. But she, lying there serenely, doesn't feel a thing. She, breathing calmly and rhythmically, waits. She, languid and unperturbed, prepares for the real me to come walking through that door. Perhaps, she'll be waiting that way forever. Who's to say? All I know is that my turn has come and gone. And it's time for me to leave. But I'm still hoping. Thinking we might again cross paths. I spend the next few moments tracing the outlines of her body, tracing the ghost of an outline really. Pretending I can still feel the smooth, iridescent, warm-to-the-touch skin that separates outside from inside. No, I don't want to leave! I reach down and grip my penis. As one hand passes over the see-through outline of her body, the other begins to stroke my foreskin. I kiss her phantom lips, slip my tongue into her non-existent mouth, run my fingers over a ghostly clitoris that will soon swell with the rubbing of another me. And I come for a second time, watching the semen squirt onto my stomach, useless navigators drowning in air. I wipe myself clean, using the same blood-stained towel—as if that can connect us again in some way. Then I rise and dress, uncertain of what to do next.

A gust of wind blows the curtains inwards. Sends them fluttering in my direction as if greeting me with open arms. I walk over to the window and look out. It's warm and the air smells of bees. In the distance is a field filled with milkweed and clover, waving before the wind. There's someone lying in the field but I can't quite make them out. Directly below is a fenced-in backyard. A green fenced-in backyard. And in the backyard a garden. At first, it looks like an ordinary garden with ordinary flowers and fruits and vegetables. But I soon realize it isn't so ordinary after all. The flowers are skeletons. Or X-rays, at the very least. The fruits skull-and-crossbone figures. The vegetables polished femurs and ulnae. More and more are popping out of the earth all the time, shaking themselves free of the earth. As one, they turn towards me. They point towards me. They begin to drag themselves towards me, yanking out roots. I jerk back from the window, afraid they might climb the walls to get to me.

On the bed, another Giulio is making love to the woman with the grey-green eyes. They must be truly physical to each other. Truly in touch in a way only flesh can be. I see them as ephemera. How do they see me? For a moment, it seems as if the woman is looking directly at me. But no. Her eyes are glazed over and it's the moment before she climaxes. The little puffs of breath coming through her nostrils. Faster and faster. The mouth slightly open and slightly twisted. Making little grunting noises. The hands fluttering, almost out of control, by her side. The body rising and falling at an ever-increasing crescendo.

I watch for a few moments more, the voyeur in me unable to resist this uneasy alliance between solid flesh and evanescent spirit. Between one body pumping like the be-jesus between the legs of another and the ghostly remains of someplace else, the bits and pieces of some other reality. Is it some sort of battle? Or is a true joining being forged? Do I care? Is it any of my concern? Hasn't all this been a mistake? After all, I shouldn't even be here, should I? This isn't even my place. It belongs not to someone who's been told his name is Giulio—like it or lump it—but to someone who knows he is Giulio. Who feels himself Giulio body and soul without even having to think about it.

I turn and walk out of the room, making sure to ease the door shut behind me. Once back on the landing, I'm overwhelmed by a tremendous feeling of longing. Of a yearning beyond anything I've known before. Worse even than the days and weeks and perhaps months I spent in that white room, listening to a soft, calming voice intent on driving me crazy. It grips me just above the pit of my stomach and works its way up to my throat. I try to swallow it back down, try to get it back where it belongs. The feeling lasts maybe ten seconds in all. But during that time, I'm unable to move. Everything is hopeless. Every action useless. Every thought like some mocking, disgusting joke that ends up turning on itself: "Ha, ha. You asked for it, didn't you, Mr. Wanna Know It All? Please, don't let me be like the dumb animals out there, you said. You pleaded. Please, let me be able to make sense of the world. And to understand my place in it. My obviously unique and invaluable place in it. Well, here you are. Now you know what it's like to be seized by the only knowledge that counts: one day you will no longer exist. Poof. All that will be left of you are bits of someone else's memories, someone else's storytelling. If you're lucky, my boy. If you're damned lucky. Otherwise. . . . You're free to vomit now. The reflex gag action will make you feel better—while it lasts."

Whatever was holding me frozen releases me at last. And with a vengeance. Like it doesn't want me anymore. Like it has no more use for me. I stumble forward with the first gagging impulse. And then another. And another after that, coming more and more quickly. I rush back into the bathroom and barely make it to the toilet bowl, falling down before it on my knees. The bile flies out of my mouth and, yes, for a moment, I do feel better. But then I can sense more forming in my stomach. Churning and erupting. I lean over and vomit again. Nothing more than spittle this time. A dribble of watery green from my lower lip to the lip of the bowl. Sour, acidic, repulsive. I splash water on my face from the tap and then reach up for a towel to wipe it clean. I assume it's the same one I used after my bath. But it smells rank and mouldy—as if it has been hanging there a long time without being washed. I look up in the mirror. The same old me stares back. At least I can be sure of that, I tell myself. Like a decrepit stump in the middle of a swirling stream: too stubborn to give way and yet unable to reach either shore.

But I'm not some soggy old stump, half-stuck in the ground and rotting away. I can do as I please. And right now, I plan on going back into that room. I plan to work my way back to that moment of penetration. Damn right! I throw the towel down and rush out onto the landing. My hand is on the knob of the middle door, hovering above it, hesitating. Do it! What have you go to lose? I throw the door open, ready to plead my case. And stop in my tracks. The room is dark; the curtains drawn. The only light comes from some candles that flicker on top of a dresser. The bed's still there but no young delectable creature lies in it, waiting to seduce me. Rather an old woman, eyes shut, waist-length grey hair spread out on either side of her. She opens her eyes before I have a chance to retreat and signals for me to approach. I want to turn back instead, to get away from the stink of old age and death. But her hand is stretched out towards me and I have no choice but to go near. As I do so, I can hear moans and wails coming from the walls where shadows in dark clothing move back and forth.

Who are you? I ask, standing nervously by the side of the bed.

They're crying for me, you know, she says, still holding out her hands. They're waiting for me to die. They've been waiting a long time. Such a long time. But I told them. I told them I wouldn't die until I saw you again.

Well, here I am, I say rather brutally..

Sit, she says, indicating a spot on the bed beside her. I'm sure you have a few minutes to spare before you get on with your life again.

I sit, sinking into the soft mattress. The wailers approach for a moment, surrounding us, at the same time both menacing and solicitous—then retreat once more into the darkness.

Hold your horses, the woman in the bed says. You'll be pulling out your hair and gnashing your teeth soon enough.

You're my mother, right? I say. Isn't that who you are?

You know, she says, touching my cheek with her fingers, I've always been able to see things others don't see. All my life it's been that way. Visions. Omens. Signs. Dreams. Dreams are funny. They don't always mean what you think they mean. If you dream of visiting a relative back home, it could mean that relative has died. So you have to know how to make them out. Do you know what I mean?

I shake my head. She caresses my face with her rough fingers, following the curves of my forehead, my eye- and cheek-bones, my chin, my lips, my nose. Almost as if she's trying to memorize them.

Right now, she says, you're wondering what you're doing here. You're wondering what has brought you here to a dying woman's bedside.

Yes, I whisper, her caresses making me feel warm and safe, as if floating in some sort of protective liquid. The kind of caresses I don't remember getting as a child.

Well, you could be part of my dream. Or I could be part of yours. Or—she smiles—we could both be part of someone else's.

No, I say firmly. I'm not part of anyone's dream. That's not going to happen to me. I'm not letting that happen.

Good for you, she says as she takes my hand in hers. The trouble with being in someone else's dream is that there's not much future for you once that person wakes up. On the other hand, the dreamer might never wake up and then you'll live forever. Unfortunately, we don't have much choice in these things.

She leans back, still holding my hand. Then, slowly, she lets go, one finger at a time. I feel as if something's being cut.

I'm tired now, she says. It was very nice seeing you. Good-bye.

That's it? I say. Just like that?

That's it, she says.

She shuts her eyes. The wailers come out of hiding. They move forward towards the bed, their keening howls becoming more and more high-pitched, more and more hard to take. I recognize them now as aunts and great-aunts and great-great-aunts. All dressed in black; all veiled in black. They edge me out of the way; they surround the bed so that I can no longer see the woman lying there—a woman I realize I've never really known.

No! I scream—and rush forward into their midst, hoping to scatter them before they can do any more damage.

But my scream serves only to propel me out of the room, to send me tumbling once more onto the landing. I stand up and try to get back in. This time the door won't open. I beat against it with my fists. I kick at it. I lunge at it. I succeed only in tiring myself out.

Bastards! I say, sliding down to sit at the base of the door. You can't do this to me. I'll get you for this. You wait and see.

But even as I'm saying it, I realize how useless my threats are. Who am I going to get? And what can I do to them?

I turn towards the third door, the one on the far right. I can see something behind it—a bright light perhaps, trying to break out along the edges. You want me to go there, do you? Well, just for that, I won't. Just for that I'll go back down the way I came. I'll show you. I'll just retrace my steps.

I head for the stairway. An angry mob awaits me. The woman from the kitchen; the man in the basement; the little boy holding bones; the man in the wheelchair; Norma; my black-caped friend; the green-eyed young woman from the bedroom. And dozens more behind them, dozens more surging up menacingly towards me.

Get outta here, you sonovabitch! the man in the basement yells, wielding a short stick whose end is covered with dirt and dangling earthworms. Get the fuck back where you belong. Ungrateful jerk!

The others take up the chant.

Yeah, you don't belong here—and you're not wanted here! We've had enough of your kind. Who the fuck invited you anyway?

Their faces are twisted and full of hate. And they mean to do me harm. All except for the little boy. He's busy tossing bones against the nearest wall. I have no choice but to back up. They keep coming, filling up the entire landing. I want to ask how the man in the wheelchair managed to make it up the stairs but somehow it doesn't seem relevant. The truth is they've found me out. It was bound to happen sooner or later. They've recognized me as the impostor that I am. And they're right to be angry. After all, I'd be mighty pissed off if I discovered my best friend, my lover, my son was a fake. Someone whose actions—and even emotions—were carefully staged. I want to tell them I didn't mean to hurt anyone. That it was their fault really for assuming I was the person they thought I was. But it's a little late for that, isn't it? Besides, who'd believe me? Wouldn't they think it was just one more act for their benefit? Suddenly, the weeks spent on the cold and damp streets seem very inviting.

Imagine, the green-eyed woman says, spitting at me in disgust. And I even let you fuck me. I let you inside me. I let you pump your fake semen into me. She spits again. Death's too good for you. You can rot in hell for all I care.

Yeah! Norma says, pulling a switchblade from her ratty jacket and flicking it in front of me. Go to hell! Go straight to hell! Prick!

The man in the black cape holds up a sign: "And that's what happened. He turned into a nice-looking young boy with a moustache just starting to show on his upper lip."

I'm smiling sheepishly, not knowing what to say and toying with the idea of admitting the truth: Yes, you're right. I'm not who you thought I was. I should have told you before. I should have come clean right at the very start. I start to open my mouth, to repeat what I've just said to myself. But they're not about to give me the chance. They surge forward en masse—kitchen knives, wooden spoons, saws and other weapons flashing dangerously close to my face. They mean business, I can see that. They don't intend to let me go without getting their whacks in. The man in the wheelchair pushes himself up against me, trying to pin me with his aluminum rims. It almost feels as if he's wearing armor of some kind. Body armor, perhaps. Chain mail. Like some chariot-ed knight of old. I reach behind me for the door knob, feeling for it, afraid to turn my back on this collection of ex-friends and family. Someone's ex-friends and family, at any rate. The first hammer is about to strike me square on the temple when I twist the knob and fly backwards into the room. The blindingly-bright room. And, with their invitation to go straight to hell still ringing in my ears, I'm falling now, off-balance, arms flailing, eyes shut against the horrible light that's more like a probe than a guide. More like a question than a comfort. And, as I scream and fall, many things come back to me. Many, many things. Things I couldn't see before. Or that didn't make any sense. Some are falling with me; others are floating in the other direction, towards the source of the light. And I know who I am at last. I know who I've been and who I'll become. I know I've been through a version of this before: blood writing on a wall, visions of paradise, purgatory, limbo, the other side. But, at this moment, as I scream and fall amid the wreckage, the knowledge doesn't make me very happy. Not very happy at all. As I scream and fall. As I fall and scream. Amid the wreckage.

XVIII. You will land. . . .

You will land with a thud. And a temporary loss of breath as the air rushes out of your mouth. But it'll be a much softer landing than you would have expected after falling from what seems such a great height. An arm-flailing, screeching, interminable height. Once you can breathe again and straighten your baseball cap, you will look around and realize why. There is sand everywhere. White, powdery sand like that found on the finest beaches. On the lidos of this world. It sticks to everything: your pants, your shirt, your elbows, your mouth, your lips, your nose, your forehead, your eyelids. And sudden gusts of wind send it swirling into the air, to create a cloud of particles so thick you can't even see the sky. Or whether or not the sky was there in the first place.

After a few moments of lying prone and catching your breath, you will assume a squatting position and brush yourself off. The brushing off is a useless gesture. In no time you're covered again by the next gust of wind. You will ask yourself repeatedly: "Where am I? What is this place? This place so empty and featureless?"

When the wind stops, you realize it isn't so empty and featureless after all. There is sand, yes. But there are also cacti. Some looking like tortured creatures on a cross. Others towering with their arms outstretched as if on the verge of surrender. Or about to command a vast army of similarly uprooted monsters. And the occasional tumbleweed sweeps by, hurrying along in its tumbleweed way. And there is a sky. Definitely, a sky. Light blue overhead, fading to darker blue towards the horizon: a most beautiful sight if the conditions were different. You stand up at last, stretching your legs. The wind is even stronger up here, literally pushing you backwards as it gusts. You remember a movie you saw once: a stoic Buster Keaton leaning into the wind, practically horizontal at one point, and yet the pork-pie hat refusing to blow away, refusing to budge from his head. That was funny. Somehow this isn't.

You will choose a direction, preferably so that the wind's to your back, and then head off. Easier said than done. No matter which way you turn, the wind is in your face, grinding the sand into any exposed flesh. Into your very pores. Walk, you tell yourself. Or quickly get buried. You lean forward, very Buster Keaton-like, and begin to walk. When the gusts are too violent, you simply throw yourself down on the sand and wait it out. Or you try to find shelter behind a cactus, your arms wrapped around its prickly base. After what must be several hours of this, you sense that, if you don't find protection soon—or at least something to quench your thirst—you'll most likely die. Slowly, painfully, mercilessly. Clutching your stomach as it cramps like a snake pinned by the head. Already, you've stumbled across several skeletal remains: half-buried in the sand, beautifully polished, sparkling in the occasional sun. These weren't human as far as you can gather—nor of any animal you've ever seen: one with a horn protruding from the middle of its forehead; another tripod-like, topped by an almost rectangular skull covered in knobs and protrusions and what seems a single eye hole. A once-living camera, perhaps. Creatures of a dead-end evolution. Were they too suddenly stranded in this inhospitable place? Were they too suddenly left defenceless and unprotected when conditions changed? You can easily see yourself in the sand, lying face-first in the sand. You can easily see the tiny, ever-busy grains scrubbing you clean of flesh, scouring every single cavity. You can easily see the strained grin beneath your vanishing lips, the knife-like ribs, the once-fertile central valley between hip-bones, the little toe curled protectively over its neighbor. And no hand to lift you away, to reverse the process before it's too late.

You will force yourself to move on. It doesn't matter that you don't know where you're going. It doesn't matter that your nostrils and mouth and lungs are being clogged by sand, that you can't spit it out fast enough. It doesn't matter that you've been reduced first to kneeling and then to crawling and finally to slithering. None of that matters. It's important to inch forward. And so you will inch forward. Blindly, worm-like. Soon, there's little to distinguish you from the other mounds of sand. They too undulate with the wind.

They too heave and sigh and whistle and sometimes even sing the most plaintive of songs. And perhaps, entities in their own right, they too have a heart beating within them, calculating the hours, the minutes, the seconds they have left. Unable to believe it will soon all stop. Abort. Cease. Discontinue. Terminate. Unable to grasp the significance of no significance, the shifting, myriad, prismatic, impossible-to-pin-down magic come to a standstill at last. The nudge-nudge wink-wink of bonehead molecules frozen apart forever in a sea of nothing. In a nothing sea, nothing do. Nothing to be done. Save thy will. As a last testament?

You'll be counting down those seconds, those tick-tock seconds. Crawling ever more slowly towards that undesired destination. Wishing Mr. Zeno could be right after all—just this one time—and the halving would never end. Like the foreverness of God's half-acre. Or Satan's quarter-acre. Or whatever.

But that's not possible, of course. Not even an option, despite its quasi-mathematical symmetry. So you pray for the next best thing. And what might that be? Why, to go quickly and without pain, of course. In your sleep. After a full breakfast and a cup of hot coffee and a glass of Florida orange juice. Sitting up on a sofa somewhere listening to John Lee Hooker and the great-grandchildren in the yard outside. Sipping a glass of homemade wine straight from the demi-john. Having sex with a life-long lover, your about-to-expire bulk adding to the pleasure of one last orgasm, one last shot of watery, lukewarm jism that dribbles painfully away. Anywhere but here, dear God. Anywhere but here.

And you will squirm forward one more time, slithering in the shallow trough caused by your fairly insignificant weight in the sand. One last time, you tell yourself, barely moving, and that's it. The end. Finis. Done. Dropped. Kaput. But no. There's yet another squirm in you. Yet another slither. Yet another slink. You rear back, prepared to throw everything into it—into that last, final squirm to end all squirms—and butt your head against something solid. Something unshifting. Best of all: something that protects you from the wind. That keeps the sand at bay. You butt your head again to make sure it's real and not some treacherous mirage left over from a previous hallucination. Harder. A thud. A resounding thud. And you feel the shock wave reverberate through you. Like a shudder from a dying animal. You feel the solidity brace itself against you and pulse back, an echo both hollow and substantial.

It's a wall. Definitely a wall of some kind. You touch it with the palms of your hands, a wall spreading out in all directions as far as the span of your arms can reach. You press your ear against its smooth surface. A faint scratching sound ripples through—insistent, but not yet desperate. Or perhaps beyond desperation. You've heard that sound before. But you don't remember where, you can't quite place where—and, truthfully, right now you don't give a damn. Assured of its realness, you wipe the crusted sand from your eyes, unstick the lids from the secretions that have sealed them shut, and dare look up. A wall alright. Several metres high and perhaps four or five wide. Made of some sort of greyish metal that not even the sand can erode. Or hasn't until now at any rate.

You will use it to hoist yourself upright. Still not completely sure, you lean against it tentatively, lightly, expecting any moment to fall through. Perhaps only there through a sheer act of will on your part, a creation out of thin air. It holds. You watch the sand skirting either side, flying over the top as if from a slingshot—and then re-grouping behind you. It feels good, like being in the eye of the storm. Or the one spot in the universe where you can't be touched. And then, from within, the thirst and the hunger return. What good is a wall against a throat that constricts to the point where breathing itself is a chore? Or a stomach that clenches up like a fist? Is the situation now any less hopeless?

You start to grope around the wall, feeling your way towards one of the edges. Not too far, however, or you'll find yourself back in the windstream. Back in the maelstrom. Nothing there. The wall is dense, impenetrable. What was a few short moments ago a virtue is now one more obstacle. If it's any consolation, you'll die back to the wall. Clutching your throat and gripping your gut rather than curled up in a mound of sand. The wind dies down for a moment. You peek cautiously around the edge, knowing how treacherous this particular wind can be. The wall isn't a simple wall after all. It's one side of a box, a rectangular container. And then you see it. The outlines of a door. More like a ship's hatch really, with a handle instead of a doorknob. And, beside it, a circular window—or port-hole perhaps to continue the naval analogy. Across the top, you can just make out the inscription—in that kind of funny script reserved for illuminated medieval manuscripts: "Be prepared to meet thy maker." Somehow, it doesn't frighten you. You reach for the handle as, without warning, the wind picks up, gusts suddenly from zero to full force. The hail of sand, tumbleweeds and other debris drives you back, forcing you to bury your head against your chest. But you aren't about to let go. No fucking way. Not when you're this close. The wind gusts so strong it practically lifts you off the ground. Once more, hand gripping handle, rest of your body horizontal, you're reminded of sad sack Buster Keaton.

Again without warning, the wind will release you. You swing down and slam forward with all your weight against the door. It flies open on its solitary hinge and sucks you in, dumping you and a mound of sand onto the floor. Then, with the subtle sound of air pressure stabilizing, seals shut behind you. But you don't have time to worry about such things. You're concentrating instead on the odor that floods the air, the smell of warmth and sustenance and, dare your say it, salvation. Thoughts of impending closure recede as you spot a table before you, a yellow table with one chair pushed against it. On the table facing the chair sits a bowl of something. From your position on the floor, you can't quite see what that something is. But steam rises from the bowl. And that's a good sign, a very good sign. Beside the bowl, some cutlery, a glass and a corked bottle half-filled with red liquid. Above it, a shaded light, like those used in pool halls. Rubber-legged you lift yourself off the floor and make your way towards the table, fighting desperately to keep from fainting. Not now, you tell yourself. You can't do this to me now. You reach the edge of the table and slump into the chair. The chair wobbles slightly—one of its legs is shorter than the others—but not enough to unbalance you. You lean over. The bowl is brimming over with soup, little star-shaped noodles and pieces of meat: chicken would be your first guess. Your hand trembles as it inches forward to grasp the spoon. To clutch it like a vise. You dip the spoon into the bowl and, spilling a good portion along the way, bring the hot broth to your mouth. It scalds your lips, your tongue, your palate, your gullet—but you swallow it down anyway. You quickly pour yourself some of the liquid and gulp that down as well. It's wine, the color of blood and with a slightly-bitter aftertaste. But it serves to quench your thirst. After the third glass, you begin to feel dizzy. You look about the room: everything is doubled and swirling—including a bunk bed in the corner. Sleep, you tell yourself. I must get some sleep. You stand up, bumping against the light and tilting the chair over in the process. The sound echoes through the room. With the swaying light as a guide, you stumble over to the bed and fall into it, face down, arms splayed. The light continues to swing for a few moments more, sending giantish shadows against the walls. But you'll be asleep by then, a sleep that might last one night. Or a thousand. You have no way of telling.

You will awake to the sound of light scratching—and sit up at once. Alert now. Refreshed. No longer half-dead or half-crazed or half-blinded. No longer spitting out sand. A barely-remembered dream: in the middle of the night, a man in a conical cap walks right through the wall. He is carrying something. A tray of some kind. You look around. There's more food on the table: corn flakes this time and coffee and a glass of orange juice. You try the door. The handle moves up and down but it won't open. Won't even budge. You look out the porthole. Squint to look outside.

It's hard to tell at first but the air seems to be clearing. Yes, definitely. Less wind and less sand. More cacti and tumbleweeds: a blossoming in a land of prickly crucifixions. And there are birds in the sky, whole flocks of birds as far as the eye can see. Ravens. Or some other sort of blackbird. All flying in one direction. On the ground, first one then another coyote lopes into view, doing that eternal sidelong shuffle, the going-nowhere gait they share with hyenas. They also glide across the porthole, looking left and right, lifting their snouts into the air. They must be howling but you can't hear them.

Suddenly, one of the birds turns its beady eye towards you. Towards your face in the porthole. As if taking dead aim, it swerves in your direction, wings tucked by its sides, body a projectile. Faster and faster until it's little more than a blur that covers more and more of your field of vision. Until it's a black shroud, someone's silent cloak come to suffocate you in the middle of the night. You pull away with a jerk, head snapping back. It splatters at full speed against the glass, beak shattering, plume of blood flying backwards, body slumping to the ground. Shuddering.

Warily, afraid of another suicide attack, you peek out the porthole. The birds show no sign of further dive bombing; the coyotes continue by in their lackadaisical way. One of them stops for a moment to lick the blood and guts from the glass; another scoops up the bird and goes off with it dangling from its red-lined mouth.

You will lean against that window all day long as if fixed to the spot. As if this is the most important task ever performed by a human being. Towards dusk, the birds and coyotes begin to thin out. There are gaps in what has seemed until now an endless army, a vast movement forward that spans the entire desert. Those passing now bear the obvious marks of stragglers and outcasts: the limp-winged and the three-legged; the blind in one eye and the mange-eaten. They are moving slowly and in disarray, no longer with the same precision as earlier in the day. All very sad and end-of-the-universe-like. And then, with little warning, it becomes too dark to see: you're released, free to do as you please.

It's at this point you realize how hungry you are and that you haven't eaten since the previous evening. The breakfast is gone. Someone has seen to that. Now, dinner awaits you on the table. Sausages and green beans and mashed potatoes and a large bottle of beer. If you're curious about how it got there, you don't show it. Nor do you question the sink and toilet that have suddenly appeared in the far corner. All you want to do is eat and drink. And, once full, hopefully find some way out. Some way back to the real world. You don't think that's too much to ask.

The search will be fruitless. You can't find a single crack anywhere, something that will allow you to slither through. So you lie on the bed once again, staring out at the invisible sky. Just before you fall asleep, a shooting star cuts across it. A line of glitter in an otherwise suffocating blackness. But that only lasts for a moment, for the time it takes to shut your eyes.

And then they open again—as if mere seconds have passed—to a light so bright, so intense you know it can't be natural. You sit up and walk to the window. It's a street scene. Vivid. Sharp. Etched. The cracked sidewalk, the asphalt pavement, the brick houses, the sway-backed horses pulling ice wagons, the dogs leaning against fire hydrants, the people jauntily strolling by—all glowing in colors out of a child's storybook. A sign hooked between two telephone poles reads: "Welcome to Park Extension—the armpit of the universe!"

You try the door again, this time beating your fist against it and shouting out for help. Nothing. The sound echoes inside the room, bounces from wall to wall; the people continue to walk by, going about their business on what seems a perfect summer day. Perhaps one or two will stop for a moment and look around, somewhat bewildered. Or scratch their scalps. But that's the extent of it. And they'll move on again once they've established the noises are only in their heads. Suddenly, out of the left-hand corner, a young man enters the frame—shaggy-haired, somewhat dishevelled, wearing a suede jacket, worn sneakers and faded blue jeans. He's looking behind him. An older woman, her hair done back in a bun, staggers into the picture. He stops to point at her. To say something to her. You can't hear what he's saying. But you can tell he's angry. You can tell he's asking her or ordering her to leave him alone. She's reaching out for him. Her hand circles towards his face, as if to caress him. Then gathers momentum to strike him full on the cheek. He pulls back, a look of unbelief and shock on his face. She collapses slowly onto the sidewalk, bouncing like a doll. He reaches down. The wind picks up. Sand begins to blow through the breezy summer day. The sidewalk, the asphalt pavement, the houses, the horses pulling ice wagons, the dogs leaning against fire hydrants, the people jauntily strolling by—they all vanish beneath the relentless sand, washed away like silt on the edge of a riverbank. Or rather like the scribblings on a child's Magic Magnetic pad just after it has been shaken.

Unsure of what has just taken place, you turn away from the porthole. Breakfast awaits you on the table. As you head towards it, you kick something along the floor. It's a nail. Or a spike of some kind. Six or seven inches long. With a tapered hexagonal shaft. Sharp. Wickedly sharp. You pick it up and place it on the edge of the table. It glints in the sun. You eat your corn flakes, after sniffing to make sure the milk is still good. You down your juice and sip on the coffee. Once finished, you hold the spike up again, wondering what possible use it could have. Aha! You rush to the door and try to insert it into the lock. No good. It goes right through but doesn't do anything. Doesn't disengage any gears or release any bolts. Perhaps you can pry the door open with it, using it as a lever. Not a chance. You hold the spike in both hands and then, with a sudden motion, jerk it towards your heart. You stop abruptly just as the point is about to penetrate your skin. You hurl it violently against the wall. It bounces back towards you, spinning ever so slowly before it comes to rest at your feet.

You pick it up for the third time. Maybe the porthole is the weakness. Maybe you'll be able to cut away at it and make your escape. The spike doesn't even leave a mark behind. Outside, the sand is blowing full force. Idly, you press the spike against the wall. An indent appears where the surface is scratched, silver against the darker material. Holding the spike in your fist, you write out the word "HELP" in tall, jagged letters. And then realize how silly that is. Such a "HELP" could only be of help on the outside. But what else could you put on that wall? What else would make any sense? And then it comes to you—almost as if you'd thought of it yourself. So simple, it's laughable.

Held in a two-fisted grip, you'll press that spike against the wall. Nail the words to that wall:

"Giulio's mother, I will have you write in my cramped style, in my cramped, ever-so-peculiar style, Giulio's mother showed him the reality in dreams. For that, Giulio vows, she can never be forgiven, must never be absolved."

EPILOGUE: Signing off

But.

For the time being.

At this particular time.

During these intervening moments.

You.

Fall.

The Author

Born in Italy, Michael Mirolla is a Montreal-Toronto novelist, short story writer, poet and playwright. His publications include the novels *The Ballad of Martin B, The Facility, Berlin* and *The Boarder;* two short story collections, *The Formal Logic of Emotion* and *Hothouse Loves & Other Tales;* a bilingual Italian-English poetry collection, *Interstellar Distances/Distanze Interstellari;* and the poetry collection *Light and Time.* Awards for his writing include The Journey Prize Anthology; The Solange Karsh Medal; the Bressani Prize for *Berlin;* first prize, The Canadian Playwriting Competition; the Macmillan Prize in Creative Writing; and a Canada Council Arts Award. A new collection of poetry, *The House on 14th Avenue,* and a new short story collection, *Lessons in Relationship Dyads,* are forthcoming from Signature Editions and Red Hen Press respectively.

Links

Search for Leapfrog Press on Facebook

Leapfrog Press Website

www.leapfrogpress.com

Guernica Editions Website

www.guernicaeditions.com

About the Type

This book was set in Minion. Designed for Adobe by Robert Slimbach, the Minion™ font is based on classical old-style types from the late Renaissance period, but was created with current technology in mind. Rigidly straight lines and sturdy strokes give the Minion font design a gracefulness that transcends the ages.

Designed by John Taylor-Convery
Composed at JTC Imagineering, Santa Maria, CA